PLOUGHSHARES

Spring 2000 · Vol. 26, No. 1

GUEST EDITOR
Paul Muldoon

EDITOR
Don Lee

POETRY EDITOR
David Daniel

ASSISTANT EDITOR
Gregg Rosenblum

ASSOCIATE FICTION EDITOR
Maryanne O'Hara

ASSOCIATE POETRY EDITOR
Susan Conley

FOUNDING EDITOR
DeWitt Henry

FOUNDING PUBLISHER
Peter O'Malley

ADVISORY EDITORS

Russell Banks
Charles Baxter
Ann Beattie
Madison Smartt Bell
Anne Bernays
Frank Bidart
Robert Boswell
Rosellen Brown
James Carroll
Madeline DeFrees
Mark Doty
Rita Dove
Stuart Dybek
Carolyn Forché
Richard Ford
George Garrett
Lorrie Goldensohn
Mary Gordon
David Gullette
Marilyn Hacker
Donald Hall
Paul Hannigan

Stratis Haviaras
DeWitt Henry
Jane Hirshfield
Fanny Howe
Marie Howe
Justin Kaplan
Bill Knott
Yusef Komunyakaa
Maxine Kumin
Philip Levine
Thomas Lux
Gail Mazur
James Alan McPherson
Leonard Michaels
Sue Miller
Lorrie Moore
Jay Neugeboren
Howard Norman
Tim O'Brien
Joyce Peseroff
Jayne Anne Phillips
Robert Pinsky

James Randall
Alberto Ríos
Lloyd Schwartz
Jane Shore
Charles Simic
Gary Soto
Elizabeth Spires
Maura Stanton
Gerald Stern
Mark Strand
Christopher Tilghman
Richard Tillinghast
Chase Twichell
Fred Viebahn
Ellen Bryant Voigt
Dan Wakefield
Derek Walcott
James Welch
Alan Williamson
Tobias Wolff
Al Young

PLOUGHSHARES, a journal of new writing, is guest-edited serially by prominent writers who explore different and personal visions, aesthetics, and literary circles. PLOUGHSHARES is published in April, August, and December at Emerson College, 100 Beacon Street, Boston, MA 02116-1596. Telephone: (617) 824-8753. Web address: www.emerson.edu/ploughshares.

ASSISTANT FICTION EDITOR: Nicole Hein. EDITORIAL ASSISTANTS: Hannah Bottomy, Kristoffer Haines, Michael Homler, and Jill Owens. PROOFREADER: Jean Hopkinson.

POETRY READERS: Christopher Hennessy, Sean Singer, Tracy Gavel, Joanne Diaz, Aaron Smith, Michael Carter, Jennifer Thurber, and January Gill. FICTION READERS: Darla Bruno, Laurel Santini, Elizabeth Pease, Kathleen Stolle, Wendy Wunder, and Eson Kim.

SUBSCRIPTIONS (ISSN 0048-4474): $21 for one year (3 issues), $40 for two years (6 issues); $24 a year for institutions. Add $5 a year for international.

UPCOMING: Fall 2000, a fiction issue edited by Gish Jen, will appear in August 2000. Winter 2000–01, a fiction and poetry issue edited by Sherman Alexie, will appear in December 2000.

SUBMISSIONS: Reading period is from August 1 to March 31 (postmark dates). All submissions sent from April to July are returned unread. Please see page 224 for a description of the guest editor policy and for detailed submission policies.

Back-issue, classroom-adoption, and bulk orders may be placed directly through PLOUGHSHARES. Microfilms of back issues may be obtained from University Microfilms. PLOUGHSHARES is also available as CD-ROM and full-text products from EBSCO, H.W. Wilson, Information Access, and UMI. Indexed in M.L.A. Bibliography, American Humanities Index, Index of American Periodical Verse, Book Review Index. Self-index through Volume 6 available from the publisher; annual supplements appear in the fourth number of each subsequent volume.

The views and opinions expressed in this journal are solely those of the authors. All rights for individual works revert to the authors upon publication.

PLOUGHSHARES receives support from the Lila Wallace–Reader's Digest Fund, the Massachusetts Cultural Council, and the National Endowment for the Arts.

Retail distribution by Bernhard DeBoer (Nutley, NJ), Ingram Periodicals (La Vergne, TN), and Koen Book Distributors (Moorestown, NJ). Printed in the U.S.A. on recycled paper by Edwards Brothers.

CONTENTS

Spring 2000

Cover painting:
Mother & Daughter—The Chat
by Mary Behrens
C-print on Sintra, 48″ x 60″, 1998

Ploughshares Patrons

This nonprofit publication would not be possible without the support of our readers and the generosity of the following individuals and organizations.

Introduction

Just one of the many delights of putting together this issue of *Ploughshares* had to do with the sense of discovery I experienced as I came upon submission after submission which challenged, and changed, my notion of the world.

However familiar I might have been with the work of my colleagues in Princeton University's creative writing program—on whom, despite the serious risk of being charged with nepotism, I called for papers—I was unprepared for the range and restlessness they continue to bring to making sense of themselves in the world, sometimes in genres with which they're not primarily associated. I think particularly of the short story by Russell Banks, the extract from a novel by his fellow professor emeritus, Edmund Keeley, of Toni Morrison's song lyrics, of Joyce Carol Oates's short play, of the selection of stunning aphorisms by James Richardson, of the poem by A. J. Verdelle.

Add to all of this spectacular new prose fiction from Lan Samantha Chang, James Lasdun, Lynne Tillman, and Edmund White, poems by Mary Jo Bang, Yusef Komunyakaa, Laurie Sheck, Renée and Theodore Weiss, Susan Wheeler, and C. K. Williams, translations of Quasimodo by Jonathan Galassi, and one has some little sense of the vibrancy of the program with which they've all been associated in the academic year 1999–2000, a year in which we celebrated the sixtieth anniversary of its founding in 1939.

Also associated with the Princeton creative writing program are two recent students of mine, Troy Jollimore and Emily Moore, whose work I'm delighted to be able to bring to a wider audience. Another two of my ex-students find their way in here, Cathy Bowman of Columbia University School of the Arts, where I taught briefly some years ago, and Meredith Drum of the Bread Loaf School of English, where I've taught for the last few summers.

I have to confess that I wasn't quite sure what to expect of the unsolicited work on which I drew for the other fifty percent of this edition of *Ploughshares,* since there's always the chance that the season might not be a good one. So it was with relief that, yet again, I found so much work of such remarkable vigor and variousness.

Despite that variousness, one may point to at least one widespread trait in both the prose fiction and poetry included here. It is an increasing tendency to synthesize the traditional and the torn, the formal and the fractured, in ways that no longer seem gimmicky but absolutely germane to the business of what I referred to earlier on—writers "making sense of themselves" in a world at once traditional and torn, formal and fractured.

That synthesis of the familial and the fissured, neatly encapsulated in the cover image by Mary Behrens, is one in which I hope you, too, will find "a momentary stay against confusion."

Gregoriou

My cousin does a wheelie in a muddied Mustang, radish red,
parks askew at Quito's, a clam bar where we drink beer,
pine the days of seminary, LSD, Jimi Hendrix playing
Strasbourg, the hours when all the Howes were stick-style
architects, and every waterfront dry goods was built
on ballast rock from Slave Coast turrets. We see *Amistad,*
we look at Gilded Age graffiti: a drawing of a white man
with a handlebar mustache from 1835, when the African
town of New Goree was razed to the ground for shoes.
Katrina's come to make a film about the colors of the heart,
so we walk past hoists, barrels, leg irons, every kind
of torture tool from Positano, to see our slave and slaver
ancestors, a cry felt deep, exploded out upon a world
that talks up medicine for corns or mouthwash mints.
On a transistor radio, you can hear BRU, which just
now plays reggae from Montego Bay, and a song
comes up upon the wind off Bristol Harbor, *Gregoriou,*
gregarious, the cleft palate and stammer suddenly
lift from all manner of talking, and love and sin stand
equally holy in the light that a mother of God streams in,
and each of our ancient maids and ministers is blessing us.

Black Magic

According to William James, there are laws in psychology. If you form a picture in your mind of what you would like or wish, and you hold that picture long enough, you produce what you are thinking.

In this way monks in certain Himalayan monasteries manifest women out of thin air while balancing cups of steaming gooseberry tea on their cocks.

I understand this now and all the laws of psychology.

And how my thoughts have been traveling beneath your skin. Sometimes you hear them in dreams or at dusk like the drip of a faucet or the evening news. You can't rest at all, much less sleep.

Of course, you might try to resist, but it's as hopeless as a prayer, clinging to the impossible.

In a matter of minutes, you're lifted from the bed or couch and out on the streets, your dress quivering in the wind like a loose sail. Strangers watch you go.

They don't know how it happens. A woman suddenly following the darkened streets, perhaps even flying on wings.

Nor do they understand the danger of it, and that it is I who am to blame.

Or how it feels to fly, the fear, the lack of control, that sensation like new teeth cutting into the shoulder blades.

When you arrive, knocking on my door, there's always that first moment when you might plummet from the air, when you feel my thoughts wash over your body like a loving glance or a cold stare.

And I know, for just an instant, you've become a mere figment of my imagination, or a silhouette, lit by my mind. Or my own sorrow.

I even know what you fear. The day I will say to myself, *This woman is not all she's cracked up to be.*

The day you'll think, *This man is a real son of a witch.* And the first flicker of anger singes our skins.

That's always the beginning, the taste of bitterness and salt when we first lick the surface of our tiny black hearts.

Ham Paints a Picture to Illustrate
an Early Lesson: O Trauma!

He remembered the dog bite. The door
opened and under the host, the hostess,
their faces unfrowned, both dressed in brown,

the dog. And happy to be seen
by a boy such as that. So small.
And so sudden. A bite

as a blur, a blow, pierce puncture red-wrought and tears.
Were there? The highest ideal of unwelcome
and now denuded of calm, air ripe with arrested attention,

yes, tears, one for each tooth mark arrayed in two rows.
Formally speaking, one step to the side
of the rhetoric of sympathy. The terrier tense and shut off

now from the party had had his six shots, had he not?
He had but what
of the boy—wee fellow—memory now marred by what
    can't be extracted

as there is no such instrument no so sharp a knife,
no drug nor attar into which it will meld
a marbleized batter, so pretty the cake.

The party keeps on, its snug details melted
to a telling without any tale
only pain out of nowhere to no one he now knew

but one he had been. So it was, so it is.
Heedless hallucination
(re)seeded in a narrative setting.

Dog. Bite. The sublime scenery
of host and hostess, the mother
a diminutive presence, protectress unforgiven

for the lapse. What is done to one.
Something. Terrible. That pain must be
endured alone. The residue

of a certainty residing as the remote so-called
(recalled) picture. Image, can one say? One can say anything
one likes but here the less said the better, he said

to himself, no longer speaking
of what can be bloodied but something less liquish,
love—oh, what a word!

Quality Time

Tires crunch against the crushed stone driveway, and a flash of headlights crosses Kent's bedroom window, waking him from a light sleep. But he wasn't asleep, he tells himself. Merely resting, eyes closed. Listening. Just as, when Rose was still in high school, he lay in bed after midnight and listened for the sound of a car—his, or the current boyfriend's, her girlfriend's father's car, sometimes even his ex-wife's car—bringing Rose home to his house, where she spent the weekend, Kent's every-other-weekend, or her spring-break week, or her two-week midsummer visit. In his house in his town, his turn to be the custodial parent.

Quality time, they called it. He would greet her at the door and make sure she wasn't drunk or high or sad, and when she was suffering from any of those conditions, he tried to treat her condition rationally, calmly, realistically. Kent was a physician, a trained scientist, as he thought of it, and also a man of the world. He knew what kids were dealing with out there. He sympathized. Even today, a decade later and more of an administrator now than a physician, Kent still sympathizes.

He hears the thump of Rose's clunky Doc Martens against the front deck, the jingle of the house key, and the slammed door. In three months Rose will be thirty, and she still slams the door when she comes in, no matter how late the hour. And Kent still checks the car for scratches and dents the morning after she borrows it. Especially this car, his brand-new Audi 3000, silver and sleek—his sixtieth birthday present to himself. He's already reminding himself to examine the car in the morning before he leaves for the office, so he won't discover the ding in the fender or the broken taillight late in the afternoon in the clinic parking lot, which is where she'll insist it must have happened, since she has absolutely zero recollection of any fender-bender occurring on her watch. He'll accept that. He'll have to. He turns on the bedside lamp, gets out of bed, and walks to the closet. But she'll be lying. Or worse, she won't really know one way or the other how it happened, and won't care, either. He pulls his bathrobe over his pajamas and pads barefoot down the hall to the kitchen.

"Hey, babe. Nice time?" he says and plucks a bunch of purple grapes from the fruit bowl on the breakfast table. She's sprawled at the table, thoughtfully drinking milk from a half-gallon container. Kent likes this kitchen, the only truly up-to-date, architect-designed room in the house. It's an orderly arrangement of stainless steel, ceramic tile, overhead pot-racks, and butcher-block islands. He had it renovated top to bottom back when he first got serious about gourmet cooking and enjoys telling people that the kitchen is state of the art. The rest of the house is more or less the way it was when he bought it fifteen years ago, the year after the divorce. Since then, though he's enjoyed several long-term romances with women, good women his own age, marriage-able women, he's not shared his house with anyone—except his daughter. Hasn't wanted to. A nineteen-fifties, mid-level mafia capo's suburban ranch, is how Kent likes to describe the house to strangers.

He pops the grapes one by one into his mouth. He's been unmarried now for nearly as long as he was married, and the fact freshly surprises him. He drops the grape stem into the trash compactor.

"I wish you'd use a glass," he says evenly. Julia, his ex-wife, gave her that habit—drinking orange juice, milk, whatever, straight from the carton.

"Sorry, Pops, I forgot. It's been a while," Rose says. She shrugs and smiles up at him, sheepishly, or maybe mockingly, he's not sure which. It hasn't been that long since she last visited him, has it? Barely half a year.

She stands and crosses to the glassware cabinet, where she takes out a tumbler and fills it, leaving the carton on the counter. Rose is a tall, large-boned woman with burgundy-colored, shoulder-length hair. Her skin comes from her mother—skin so smooth and strikingly pale it seems washed in a hazy-blue light. When Julia was Rose's age, he remembers, she tied her hair back the same way and in summer favored sleeveless, V-neck blouses. Julia then, like her daughter now, showed as much face, throat, and arms as possible. If you've got it, she used to say, show it.

Kent doesn't know how Julia does her hair now or if her skin is still as beautiful—he hasn't seen her close-up in over seven years. He imagines that she's changed in that time as much as he and in most of the same ways. In seven years your whole body replaces itself, cell by cell.

He picks up the milk carton and returns it to the refrigerator. "So how was it tonight, with your old pals?"

"Okay," she says. "It was fun." Then, "*Not,* actually. Not okay. Not fun."

"Oh? Why?"

"Eddie and Jeanette and Tucker and Sandy? They're not my old pals. Not really. And they're married, they're couples, et cetera. And they're definitely on the boring side. Tep-id."

"They are?" he says in a low, sad voice. He wants to let his disappointment show without having to say it.

"Yeah. I didn't even know them, you know, till after the divorce. I mean, I *knew* them, we hung out a lot when we were teenagers, but it was mostly summers, Dad. A few weeks at a time."

He understands. It has to be hard for her, five hours on a Trailways bus to visit the old man every six months or so for a long weekend or maybe a week. Then being alone with him at his house (her house once, as he often points out, but, as she insists, not hers anymore), until he fears he's holding her against her will, so he starts pushing her to go out on her own, go ahead, borrow the Audi, visit some of her old pals. Most of the local people her age, because they've not left this small, upstate town for more promising climes, have married one another and have settled for much less than Rose wants for herself. She's right. They *are* boring.

Rose is an artist, a sculptor who has already had two one-person shows of her work, the first at Skidmore in Saratoga Springs, where she went to college, and the other at a small gallery in Litchfield, Connecticut, where Julia lives. Julia and her second husband, Thatcher Clarke, the executive director of the clock and watch museum there, helped arrange it. When Julia first met Thatcher, a few months before her divorce from Kent became final, he was the director of the Adirondack Arts Council and had already been hired to run the clock and watch museum down in Litchfield, one hundred twenty miles to the south. Within weeks of the divorce, Julia followed him there. Rose went with her. Because of the schools. That's when the need for quality time arrived.

Kent honestly believes that Ol' Thatch, as he calls him, is perfect for Julia, and he's been a good stepfather for Rose. He's a hale fellow well-met, in Kent's words, and a liberal New England Republican. Kent, on the other hand, is proud to be neither. He spoke with Ol' Thatch briefly at Rose's high school graduation, renewed their slight acquaintance when she graduated from Skidmore, and saw him a third time last fall at the Skidmore show.

Julia didn't attend the opening. She was at a health spa in New Mexico, Rose explained. Was she okay? Health-wise? "Oh, sure," Rose assured him. "It's about weight. As usual." Julia had mailed the spa her fifteen-hundred-dollar deposit months earlier and didn't want to lose it, so Rose told her to go, for heaven's sake. She could see Rose's new work on her own anytime. Two months later, Rose had the show in Litchfield.

Rose kisses her father on the cheek, says goodnight, and saunters down the hall toward her room, flipping off lights as she goes. Her bedroom is situated on the opposite end of the house from Kent's master bedroom. It was originally meant to be guest quarters, but the first weekend Rose spent with him in his new house, when she was fifteen, Kent turned the guest bedroom, dressing room, and bath over to her. He did it casually, as if it were something that occurred to him only when it was happening, but it was long-planned and for him a memorable event. It was his first chance to feel like a father, a real father with a house large enough to give his teenaged daughter her own bedroom suite, where she could play her music and watch TV and talk on her own phone without interfering with his music, TV, and phone. He was no longer a middle-aged single guy subletting a semi-furnished garden apartment in a complex filled with young professionals. He'd hated that. He was a proper family man now. His house, his daughter's rooms, and her regular, ongoing presence at his house proved it.

He needed that visible evidence of paternity, and he believed that Rose did, too. The divorce was harder on her, he feels, than either Julia or Rose herself is willing to acknowledge—Julia because she still feels guilty for the several, careless little love affairs that led up to the divorce and ostensibly caused it, and, too, because she was the one who afterwards moved away; and Rose because she doesn't want her parents to worry about her any more than they already do.

It wasn't Julia's dalliances, though, that caused the divorce, or her removal to Litchfield that heightened the pain of it for Rose. And Kent knows it. As the years pass, some things in life do get simpler, and Kent's divorce from Julia was becoming one of those things. No, it all came down to the simple fact that he grew up, and she didn't, and then wouldn't. And because she had plenty of inherited money, she's never had to. She didn't need Kent's money or proximity to raise their child, she could do it on her own, and mostly, that's what she did. There's no way, of course, that he can tell this to Rose or Julia. Not now. They'd think he was criticizing them, and he wasn't.

Kent washes Rose's milk glass in the sink, places it into the dish rack, and switches off the overhead light. He steps into the darkened sitting-porch just off the kitchen—he can't remember if he locked the door to the backyard. The flagstone floor is cold against his bare feet, when suddenly it's as if he's walking on gravel or broken peanut shells. Popcorn, maybe. Beads from a broken necklace? He gropes beside him in the dark, until his hand finds a floor lamp.

It's birdseed! A wide trail of sunflower and wildflower seeds and cracked corn spills from the pantry behind him, where he stores a hundred-pound bag of mixed birdseed in a large galvanized trash can. The trail crosses the porch to the door leading outside. Mornings over his second cup of coffee and evenings over his first scotch and soda, Kent often sits out here on the glider and watches the birds flutter greedily over the three large birdfeeders hanging from the maple tree. There are finches, both purple and gold, pine siskins and grosbeaks, cardinals and phoebes. Once he saw an indigo bunting and was so excited he shouted, "Look!" but he was alone. His shout, even through the glass, scared the bunting, and it flew away and didn't return.

He stares down at the birdseed scattered over the slate floor, and he feels his neck and ears redden. She must have refilled the feeders sometime earlier tonight, and instead of bringing the feeders into the pantry and filling them there, which is how he does it and has demonstrated for her any number of times, she carried the seeds, scoop by scoop, across the porch and out the door, spilling as she went. That's so damned typical! And, of course, since she never sees disorder anyway and didn't see the stuff scattered across the floors of the porch and pantry, she didn't think to clean it up. Never crossed her mind. He strides down the hall to Rose's end of the house, snapping on lights as he goes.

He knocks firmly on her door. Not with anger, for while he is exasperated, he's not angry. He's confused. He can admit that much. After all these years, he still doesn't understand why she can't or won't remember what he tells her to do, what he asks her to do, what he wants her to do, when she's in his house. When she's in his *life,* for heaven's sake. She acts as if, for her, his life doesn't exist, or if it exists at all, it doesn't have any meaning. He can't bear that.

She opens the door. She's wearing green and blue plaid flannel pajamas and has her toothbrush and toothpaste in hand. "You haven't gone to sleep yet, have you?" he asks evenly.

"I haven't made my evening ablutions yet," she says smiling. Then she sees his expression. "What's the matter?"

"The birdseed, Rose. You spilled it all over the porch floor."

She wrinkles her brow and stares at her father's face, not quite getting what he's after. "I did?"

"Yes."

"Sorry. I . . . I wasn't aware . . . ," she trails off. "The birdfeeders were almost empty. You want me to clean it up . . . now?"

"If you don't mind."

She sighs audibly. "O-kay."

Kent turns and walks purposefully back to his side of the house, not stopping until he's inside his bedroom and has closed the door, extinguished the light, and has got himself under the covers in bed. He's breathing rapidly, as if he's just climbed three flights of stairs. His heart is pounding, and adrenaline is rushing through his body. He knows what's happening to his body, he's a doctor, after all. But *why* is it happening? Why is he fuming over such a trivial offense? Why even view it as an offense in the first place? Must he take *personally* everything his daughter does wrong?

In the morning, Kent leaves for the office before Rose wakes. There are no dents or scratches on his Audi. He feels guilty for last night, not because he did or said anything to hurt her, but because he *was* angry, when clearly something else was called for.

He's not sure what, but he knows that anger was useless to them both. Useless and therefore offensive somehow. Around ten, he telephones the house, and she picks up. "I wondered if you'd like to meet me for lunch downtown," he says, a little shy and stiff.

"Sounds great!" She's chewing food, he can tell, and is probably still in bed in her pajamas, flopped in front of the TV, working her way through the lox and bagels he bought especially for her visit.

"Want me to come by the house and pick you up?"

"No, I'll ride the bike! It's gorgeous out, and I need the exercise. I've been a lump all week."

They agree to meet at his office at one. At a quarter to one, Kent walks out the door of the clinic, leans against the railing of the front steps, and looks along the street uphill to his right, where he knows that Rose in a few moments will come into view pedaling her old bike, the blue Raleigh three-speed that he bought for her the summer she turned fourteen. She already owned a bike, a present on her twelfth birthday from both Mom and Dad, but he bought her the Raleigh himself so that, after the divorce, she could ride from her mother's house to his whenever she wanted, he told her. Then Julia moved. Or from his house to the office, he assured her, where they could meet for lunch on Saturdays when he had to work. She rode from his house on Ash Street to Main and then cruised ten blocks along Main to the long, curving hill that flattened and straightened where it passed in front of the clinic. He remembers October leaves skidding across the sidewalks and streets, and the sky was deep blue. He liked to wait on the steps outside, just as he is doing today, and every time he saw her pedal around that far curve with a wide, excited grin on her face and her auburn hair flying behind her in the rippling sunlight, his chest filled with joy and with an inescapable sadness, and he could barely keep his eyes from flooding with tears. He knew what gave him the joy—she did; he loved her, and the joy proved it—but he did not know what caused the sadness.

Here she comes now, a beautiful young woman in jeans and mint-green sleeveless T-shirt, wearing sunglasses, and smiling broadly at the sight of her father. He stands on the clinic steps with arms folded, still a hundred yards away from her, and she lifts her right hand high in the air and waves.

He waves back, smiles, and feels his chest tighten and buckle with emotion. He has never felt as proud of Rose as he does at this moment. It's the simplicity of her beauty and her sincerity, he decides. That's what makes him proud of her. They are qualities of body and character, qualities of *self*, that for unknown reasons have been invisible to him until this moment. He doesn't ask why he never saw them before. Instead, he wonders why they should have suddenly become visible.

Because she is at hand, yet still far away, is his answer. But coming nearer by the second, and nearer, when suddenly, to avoid hitting something on the road that he can't see, a piece of broken glass, perhaps, she swerves the bike out into the middle of the street and puts herself between an oncoming UPS truck and a Volvo station wagon bearing down behind her. Kent reaches toward her with both arms, his mouth wide open as if to shout, but he can't break his silence, he can't even say her name, and she swerves a second time, this time cutting in front of the UPS truck and off Main Street onto a narrow lane on the opposite side, where she disappears.

The UPS truck passes Kent nonchalantly, as if the driver has noticed nothing out of the way, as if he's not seen anyone in danger for a very long time, and the Volvo station wagon passes in the other direction as normally as cars have passed all day, the woman driver chatting with the passenger, her husband, perhaps, or a client to whom she's about to show a house. Then, on his right and across the street, Rose emerges from behind a high hedge on the corner of Main, pedaling her blue Raleigh with ease and obvious pleasure. She's still smiling and is close enough now to call to him and be heard, "Hey, Dad! What a day, huh?"

Kent rushes across the street and grabs her bicycle by the handlebars and stops it dead. Rose's face drops and tightens. Her father is panting, red-faced, sweating.

"Jesus, Dad, what's the matter?" she asks, her voice rising in fear. "Are you okay?"

"*Why?* Why do you do this to me? To *yourself!* Why do you do it to yourself?"

Rose lets go of the handlebars. She reaches forward and places her hands on her father's shoulders, as if she is the parent and he the reckless child. "Dad," she says. "Stop."

"*Why?*"

Then, calmly, patiently, with a detachment that's incomprehensible to him, she explains. "I do it because what you do is violent, and it makes me violent, too. That's why." The two of them stand there with the blue bicycle between them, traffic whizzing by in the background.

"What? It's *my* fault?"

She sighs, and then she tells her father what he needs most to know, but has always seemed incapable of knowing: that his loving kindness and intimacy draw her close to him, but only for him to reject her—because of her sloppiness, her carelessness, her disorder. She reminds him of last night's confrontation over the spilled birdseed. She tells him that he should have let it go till morning. "I'm twenty-nine, Dad. Leave me a note. I'd have cleaned it up this morning." He spoiled their earlier moment in the kitchen, she says, which, if he had left her alone, would have helped her deal with her little failure later in a useful way. "In a way that wouldn't have scared you. You don't know, but it's what I've been doing for years," she says.

"What have you been doing for years?"

"Things that would scare you, Dad. Only this time you saw it."

Side by side, they walk along the sidewalk, uphill away from the office. Rose keeps one hand on the handlebars, steering the bike, and the other on her father's slumped shoulder. "I'm not angry at you," she says, sounding distant and almost scientific. "Not anymore." She understands his needs. Her needs, however, are different, and it's her mother, she says, who's shaped her needs. Not him.

"Your mother?"

"Dad, Mom is like my hollow double," she says. "My absent self. Not you. You're my father." All these years he's treated her as if she were like him, she explains, instead of like her mother. And consequently he's dealt with her as if she had his needs instead of her mother's. Rose smiles at him, but from a great height.

It's only a flash of awareness, as if a darkened room were lit for a second and then dropped into darkness again, but Kent sees how vain and cruel he's been. He sees that he's been a man completely opposed to the man he thought he was. And as surely as he lost her mother fifteen years earlier, he has lost Rose now, and for the same reason. He knows nothing of his daughter's needs, because he knew nothing of her mother's.

He says to Rose, as they turn off Main Street onto Ash, "Was I wrong, to divorce your mother? To leave you?"

"No," she says. "You weren't. But you shouldn't have tried to keep her through me. And me through her," she says. "Now you've lost us both."

"You'll never come to visit me again, will you?"

She shakes her head no. "I'm sorry. I think this has been the end of everything between us. But we'll see." She tells him to go on back to his office. She'll leave the bicycle in the garage and call a cab to take her to the Trailways station.

He stops, and she continues on.

Persephone and the Man of Letters

Of A. Of the abracadabra triangled
below the navel's amulet. Of the underworld
still with me as I drive all night to you
following a red Trans Am,
my beacon and talisman.
Before me the mysterious lands of corn and soy.
Behind me our Atlantic's salty winds.
O glorious Susquehanna and wild grasses!
Here in the pearl beads of your abacus. I am
first an old-fashioned long division,
then an algebra without numbers
only spheres and stars. You are all

Of B. The broadest letter. Two blooms
held with a bandit's knot. Wonder split
to the very beginning of your because.
Fireflies troll in slow-mo on a labial mute,
the bow-stringed scales of Spring's new moon.
Fireflies become a thousand eyes, packed
in the honey-filled magnavox—i.e., the sky.
Quiet now, I see 26 trees and 26 varieties
of warblers speaking to me. They have information
for me. As my body shoots straight through

C. The fastest letter. I'm trying to slow down.
To count slowly. One, Mississippi. Two,
Fra Lippo Lippi. Three, Krispy Kreme. Four, my
grandma's cornbread recipe. Come a
little closer, and I'll tell you the one
ingredient I always leave out. And it starts with

D. Of door number 3. The delta
where I backstroke the distance between
the devil's trap and the deep blue.
Some call it a dance. Whatever the term
is for what we are doing, it feels
as if wind and matter had not been invented.
Listen! An owl or maybe a cuckoo resurrected.
Bird of knowledge. There's nothing
smart about this night.

Of E. Of Bee Vamp. Of humidity. Of day-old coffee. And fries
extra crispy. Of eight ball. Of turning forty. Of each other. Of
easy street.

Of F. What's spelled out after the fifth is taken.
At 4 a.m. the fist greased with a train whistle's resin.
Insects horned and drunk on berry liqueur. The stars
above shavings from de Sade's festive board.

Of G. Of the gimme cap. Of the grooves in vinyl where we sing of
    graves and worms and epitaphs. The heaviest letter.

Of H. I am sorry, husband, it is Spring, and I must leave you for a
    time in hell.

Of I, J, K, and L. All private.
A package of pomegranate seeds.

Man of letters.

Of the N in the new-dropped foal.

Of the O in armadillo. And the silver buttons in the 501's.

Of the P. Printed. Transcribed. Vertebrated.

Of Q. Quote—that tail that my heart spins on—unquote.

Of R. The months when oysters are eaten. Including Jurn, Jurlie, Ourgust, and Mare.

Of S. Somewhat immaterial. Smart as sparrow eye. Dumb as saliva.

Of the T-shaped sphere-hook that caught
the flounder that we grilled at low tide
on the beach so many years ago.

Man of U. Sans serif.

Of V. The votive set in the crux of a camphor tree.

Of woadwaxen. The dyer's green weed.

And the X-axis. And the archaic yegg.

Of Z. And all that razzmatazz. Of the single snare's zone time in the zebra-striped Z-Bar. And it's fun to talk in Dietrich's accent, "Your eyes are zee stars above zee Baltic," as your forefinger undoes the zip code. Again. Spring. What with all you have laid out for me, beloved, as I climb up and down this ladder that is my life's sentence.

1979

I. Ancient Playground

I'm standing idly by while Denis
or "Dino" McCarthy (him of the wire-rimmed specs
and the hair like a set of loosening springs)
unzips his army pants, extracts his penis,
and pisses stoutly into Chuck Gilheany's brown quart bottle
    of flattening
Bud. He sleeps for now but soon will wake and drink. I've only
    just had sex

of a kind with Romana Barran in the convent
doorway of our alma ma'
and am still adhesive with the dried distillate.
Magnolias have blossomed here with their smell of unripened
    melons.
I'm licking each finger of my right
hand, drunk in the park with these fledgling felons.
By now she's home at her parents' second apartment
brushing her braceless teeth, stripped of her training bra.

II. Mt. Sinai

Unless that was the night when the Fungus
Brothers flipped onto one of the quartzite
chess tables three bags of a cocaine so crosscut
and stepped on that it found, among the connoisseurs,
no takers; the very night
I waited in the back seat of a hand-shammied bootblack Duster
with Joey Ola and Brian Daly, each of us
set after this girl with a body like a bowlful of tit

who was inside visiting her cancerous or, maybe, car-wrecked
uncle. We'd picked up her and her ugly
friend at Mimi's. I was turning over in my mind
an image I had recently purloined
from *The Year of the French.* The bright black hood reflected
the unblinking neon word EMERGENCY.

III. 84th and York

And then I said nothing
as this chimp-faced Bowery Boy with a homemade blood
blue tattoo of a cross on the back of his hand
three times touched the tip of a cigarette to the polyester blend
windbreaker Stephanie Ryalls wore knotted
around her ample waist. And then I stood

by. In the parish of St. Stephen of Hungary.
Stephanie Ryalls and her friend Irene—
feathered hair, tight white pants, eyeshadow blue as
     a morpho's wing
and dusty—a pretty guttertongue
who'd been raped summerlong
by her rusticated uncle and cousin
and had returned to the city
prepared to fuck anything.

IV. Pier 99

But enough about all that, enough
already. I'd rather fix my mind's eye on
a potted fern hung in smoke and breath
above the bar at Cobblestones (formerly Carroll's),
on the crazed shadow it gives across the skin
of Jill Holtzman, leaning close to hear me, and her tough
but gorgeous friend Deirdre Dowd, the youngest of six girls,
six beauties who have spent the '70's as a sort of private bakery
     of love and death

so steady is their transit between conception and abortion.
This pair have just come from Studio 54 or The Mint.
I'm too hammered to make the connection.
In the morning I'll meet Lenny B. at the Hudson River helipad,
looking like I've downed a thousand pints of lint,
then catch a ride to the beach with Mom and Dad.

v. 12 Ocean Boulevard

That you've got to go down
on a lobster is one thing he taught me that afternoon—
the emptied shells on the garden table so clean and filled
     with light
when he was done
with them the small vaults of the buttery white
interiors glowed red as the tortured defunct exoskeletons—

that you should go down on all things living and desired.
The 3rd of July. His face ashine
from what he'd pushed it into. Ebony and ivory; an opera
of *Lolita;* Humbert Humbert singing "Hey Big Daddy
you're driving me batty"—
he'd put that one aside but would try it again if I'd
do the libretto. Would I? Lust, I guess. Life. I'm taking it all as
     opera buffa.
I have my eye fixed on some distant mine.

Broth of Heaven

M r. Tao had outlived his wife but that didn't bother him, he always said. In time he would catch up to her in heaven. Each day he waited calmly in his chair. The winter light moved square by square across the tile floor. On Friday afternoons when I came by he looked at me through cataracts as blue as porcelain and shrugged, as if to say, "Why do you visit me? I have no interest in food."

I don't think he suspected why I always sat so long with him. I wanted him to eat, of course, but my other reason was a selfish one. He made me less uncomfortable than the other residents because his room never smelled. At eighty-five years, and ninety-eight pounds, he had the breath of a young man. He did not give off the odor of someone rotting from within. The air that hung about his bed and chair was clean and healthy.

"Not even a nice *dianxin*?" I asked, one bleak afternoon in mid-December. "There's a new restaurant on Canal Street that makes the most delicious vegetarian dumplings. They're as pure as monk's food."

"Good for the monks."

None of the other Chinese residents at my church retirement home had as indifferent an appetite as Mr. Tao. It was from talking with them that I had thought up the idea for my service contribution: to supplement their meals with odds and ends from downtown. Some lived in suites with kitchens and depended on me for fresh tofu. Some craved an occasional takeout order of softshell crab. I would get their orders and hurry away. Coming back on the train with sacks of groceries, I felt necessary, even happy.

"Not even some green tea?"

"I have everything I need."

I looked around the room. On the wall hung a lunar calendar with holidays in red, donated each year by the Xidong Bank. The shelf over the table held only a bilingual Bible in large print. In the corner next to his leather slippers sat another, smaller pair of purple slippers embroidered with pansies and geranium leaves. I never asked about them.

"I bet you could use a good meal yourself," he said.

When I looked away I saw a small cross opposite his chair, nailed on the wall where you wouldn't notice unless the door was closed.

"Why don't you answer?"

"I am not an eater," I said. "I am a cook."

"Who do you cook for?"

"My husband, when he lived with me."

"Where is he now?"

I did not know. Three years ago, one bright, cold morning in late November, he had left the house without a word. I had just made a pot of red bean porridge; he had left behind his emptied bowl and porcelain spoon.

So many meals I had made for him. When we were young, I had spent hours rolling out thin-edged dumpling skins. I had made dumplings small as pigeon's eggs, filled with savory juice that filled the mouth when they were bitten into. I had sliced red autumn peppers so perfectly that each piece cooked to the exact same sweetness. In later years, when he grew tired, I steamed him chicken with hambones in the clay pot I had inherited from my mother. I had stewed spareribs with cloves and ginger and fresh acacia honey. How was it possible that I could have cooked for him for so many years and never known what he wanted?

Mr. Tao had shifted in his chair. "I hate food," he said, and his voice was bitter and hungry.

"How can you say that?" I asked. "You are in such good health at your age because you ate well during your life."

"I was a slave to it."

His words burned angrily into the room. "Those celery hearts. That ginger pork. That broth," he said. "That broth she made, with a whole chicken breast, for flavor. The ginger sweet and fresh, sliced thin like curling paper with the knife I kept so sharp for her. The fresh egg whites swirling into ribbons. Filled with protein to keep me young. Now look at me. I am living so long because of her care. I may never see her again."

He stopped talking then. I think he had forgotten I was there. In the long silence I stood up as quietly as possible and left the room.

Origin and Ash

Powder rises
from a compact, platters full of peppermints,
     a bowl of sour pudding.
A cup of milk before me tastes of melted almonds.

It is the story of the eve in which I begin. Gifts for me:
boxes of poppies, pocket knife, an elaborate necklace
made of ladybugs.

My skirt rushing north

There is something round and toothless about my dolls.

They have no faith. Their mouth, young muscle
                         in which to cut me down.
Their pupils miniature bruises.

     I hear the cries of horses, long faces famished,
                              the night the barn burned,
their sound was the key

which opened human doors.

The day afterward, there was God and ashes everywhere.

Burnt pennies, I loved them, I could not catch them
in their copper rolling.

My mother's cigarette burns amber in a crystal glass.
I am not there
because I am in bed imagining great infernos.

Ashes skimming my deep lake.

In my story, the night the animals burned,
I kissed the servant with salty lips.

There was a spectacular explosion, a sound
        which severed the nerves, I was kind to that shaking.

        The horses,
the smell of them, like wet leaves, broken skin.

Laughing against a wall, my hair sweeps the windowsill,

thighs show themselves.

First came my body, my statue's back, then hair electric,
matches falling everywhere.
        Tucked in my pink canopy, I am plastic,
                worn cheeks grinning.

I found my little ones hiding from me, crying into their sleeves.

They are really
from a breeze, momentary, white.

When we unburied the dolls, red ants were a fantasy
feeding on them, nest of exposed veins, shrunken salted corpses.

        There is mythology planted in my mouth which is like sin.
Keep fires inside yourself.
My mother once said,
When you were a baby, I let you swim in a basin of water
until your lungs stopped. Since then, my eyes were open windows,

the year everything fell into them.

The sound of burning is like a country of cicadas hissing endlessly.
Ashes on my white dress.

Ashes in mother's hair. Ashes on my baby brother.
The streets are arid, driven toward fire.

If I hurry, I will dance with my father before the sun sets,
my slippers clicking
on a thin layer of rain.

Confetti lifts over the fairground

Confetti lifts over the fairground. Happy music, played to make us happy, slows its parade, dims as it pivots at the curb. While I hide in the copse, the outlines lighten, my skeleton, luminescent. I take the thick cup in both hands, drink urgently. Warm wind plays litter across the yard.

My company's shattered glass, a shallow receding puddle where a goldfish puffs away, where chips of eggshell shiver on the surface, color bleeds from tissue, and the sky tries to settle. I win if I'm found by the day's end.

Leaves clatter on the breezeway, tapping blind, shoaling, begging me, my frame as it locks to itself, as I swallow—to rise.

Goodbye to the Orchard

Beautiful from the get-go, we were
Incarnations of the new, and pure sex.
I'll miss that, along with the unicorns.
The organic bower of our garden grew
Into anybody's memory of a bed
Or a mattress, in a shack near a lake.
"Mistakes, like love, are to be *made,*"
You said. I hadn't thought of that.

That first autumn was easy, the liquor
Of decay headiest at noon. And the orchard,
Let's face it, had begun to resemble a casino,
All its tables rigged in our favor. The yoke
Of being cared for is what cast us out,
Not that immense, bearded librarian,
Our curator, and not our having learned
How to get on one another's nerves.

Goodbye to the orchard: green
One day, the next day blood. We know
To stiffen at a voice; how to tell the truth
From an untruth; what's sweet, what stinks.
Behind each sleeping dog, another to let lie.
Who knew an innocence taking ages to perfect
Could fall so short when time came to live?
You knew, and then you let me know.

J O H N   D ' A G A T A

Museum of American Frontier Culture and Hall of Fame

Staunton, Virginia

But what you should concentrate on is my homesickness.

All these roadmaps, tickets, thing-in-a-glass-case—

What could make you homesick, for what drive until you glimpsed an end?

Look: here they have a little Pilgrim village, a little farming lot, a small extravaganza of skirmishes.

EVERY HOUR, WEATHER WILLING, the Indians appear, run around, yell, set fire, raid, pretend to kill a young lady, leave.

Every evening with flax the young lady attaches whatever she wants to happen next onto the soaked-blank flour sacks, then waits.

The Indians appear. The Indians leave.

Flax, and now the gown taking shape, there, where the collar soon, the insinuation of a sleeve...

The Indians there, not there.

The sacks soaked free of their stamped-on trademarks.

The flax soaked up by the gown as it stretches.

The sacks undone into windows of flowers.

Or maybe filigree.

Or are they fringes?

(The Indians continuing to visit her.)

Stop here and it is *wedding dress.* Stop here and it is
tablecloth.

What do you want to see? Say where you want to go.

I want to come to a full-stop place eventually.

Want to see you looking here, and catch myself looking back, and
find between us a distance, after all, that is not so great.

And not so insignificant.

Labors of the Heart

The remarkable thing in dreams: people say what he never hears in waking. Fat. They say it to his face, not behind his back, or clear of earshot. The word is succulent in their mouths—Faaat—stretching out like the waist on his sansabelt pants. Nothing derogatory about it, only an unabashed honesty. On these mornings, for a few moments, he wakes feeling curiously relieved.

Clarence John Softitch, Pinky to his friends, at five foot eight and four hundred and eighty-two pounds on a good day, *is* fat, not large, big, or big-boned. Not hefty, husky, generous, or oversized. Nor robust, portly, or pleasingly plump. He is fat. Enormous. Corpulent. And no delicate euphemisms or polite evasions can relieve him of this knowledge when every movement, whether tying a shoe or climbing a short flight of stairs, becomes a labor of the heart.

Not that he has much to do with people in general. He lives in Clarkston, Washington, a scrappy town of twenty-odd thousand on the eastern edge of the state where the paltry rainfall encourages prickly pear in lawns and twelve percent of the population is on welfare. He works as night janitor at Loyola High School, and when most the town's folk are gathered in families for dinner, or socially at Hogan's Bar, Pinky's company is the clatter of scrub bucket, mop, and brush. For solace he has his voice—a fine, clear tenor to fill the empty rooms. He sings, *"When the moon hits your eye like a big-a pizza pie, that's amore."*

Not that he knows anything about that. *Amore,* that is.

For he is virginal, a moderate embarrassment at his age, having come to terms, he believes, with the reality that no one loves a fat man. And so he has given up on love, the daydreams, the hope, the mooning about, the unsightly chase and precipitous rejections. Until this Monday, that is, on one of his twice weekly food shopping trips, when he sees *her* in the produce aisle of the northside A & B grocery, a rutabaga under her nose, a peckish look about her mouth. She's little. A narrow, neatly planed body.

There is about her the solidity, the starkness of a lightning rod.

He finds this fascinating; more than that it stirs him in a way he's never imagined, his feet locked like a stammer, his breast tightening unlike the usual angina. But what is it about this woman? Her shoulders pinned at attention—the fierce way she sniffs out the proper rutabaga, so that he feels intimidated. Dwarfed, really. For although Pinky *knows* himself to be large— talcums each pant leg to keep his thighs from chafing, avoids chairs with arms—he's always *believed* himself small, just a tiny voice chirping on the horizon, flotsam in an ocean of flesh. He's amazed at how his vessel sloshes and wags, jiggles and rolls. The *real him* adrift inside like a buoy at high tide. He cannot imagine being of consequence in the larger world beyond bumped tables and broken chairs, the numerous bruises and insulted flesh so common that he has ceased to wonder at the many ways the world is rigged against the fat.

But standing in the grocery aisle, he knows for the first time in his forty-odd years what it means to be *struck* by love.

She passes on the rutabagas, and even as she's whisking out of produce, he's slipping the vegetable under his nose and then into his cart, perhaps as a keepsake, as he's never actually eaten one, doesn't know what to do with the thing bowling down the cart's length, tippling stacked, frozen dinners—breaded fish sticks; Hungry Man slabs of Salisbury steak, mashed potatoes, and gravy; lasagna; chicken Kiev—and the comfort foods: donut holes, potato chips, a baker's dozen Hostess Ho-Ho's, chocolate cheesecake as a chaser. A front wheel turned sideways thumps, ba bump, ba bump, ba bump, calling everyone's attention, he thinks, as he trails her to the checkout lane before he's actually ready.

He tries not to stare, but admires the efficiency of her moves. She retrieves each item with a lean elegance, and he hangs on to the cart handle, dizzy with love, half hopes she notices the rutabaga. When she leaves the store, she's burdened by six plastic sacks hanging plumb from her fists. She staggers out and pauses in the sunlight, the door frozen open at her back so that the heat wafts in and he imagines her body, that small dark column, immune to the glare of sun on concrete, her clothes dry, armpits forever fresh.

By the time he's checked out, she's gone, and as he pulls onto the street he sees her struggling down the block. He closes his teeth against the knocking of his heart and idles behind her, the wide-body Chevy wallowing like a whale in the shallows as he leans across the seat to roll down the window.

"Can I give you a lift?" he asks.

She angles a suspicious look at him—the friendly stranger—but then she stiffens her back along with her upper lip and marches on.

"Just a ride. I'm safe," he says and has to steer around a parked car.

She glances over her shoulder. "Do I look like I need help?" she says. She crooks her elbows and flexes tidy biceps, causing the plastic bags to twist in slow revolutions, and from the cotton-woods, white duff spindles down into curbside drifts, a goldfinch flits overhead—a stab of yellow and gone—and still she holds the bags high, until Pinky begins to feel *he* is that assortment of odd bulges and bumps bundled in an unsightly sack turning this way, then that.

Of course she doesn't need help, certainly not from him, and he ducks his head in apology, cheeks flushing with an old but familiar heat. What is left him is this small dignity—he touches a finger to his forehead, as if to tip a cap, and accelerates down the street as though his heart were still intact.

It's a full week before he sees her again, which is odd, because it turns out she's his new neighbor, rents the old Grieger house kitty-corner. Though given his daytime schedule of sleep and her-mitage he hasn't noticed the lights on, the mail delivery, the mowed lawn, before this moment. Curious also is how he recog-nizes her, half-concealed as she is beneath the draped branches of a weeping birch, her back to him, head tilted so that the short nap of hair twists into something like a question mark against her neck. No more clue than the spine's rigidity, the belligerence in her stance, and still Pinky's heart begins to toll. He wishes he were driving, but these last three nights he's begun an exercise pro-gram—walking the three blocks to work and back. *Morbidly obese*, he's been categorized. Morbidly. As in deadly, not sadly, which is the way he's preferred to construe it. Midway second block, he'll be winded, and by the time he reaches the school door the back of his shirt will be sweated in the early evening cool.

He'd walk by her house without stopping, but she's noticed him, turns, and by the look on her face he can tell she can't place him. He tries not to waddle, wishes he were wearing something other than Carhartt coveralls. He tips his finger to his forehead and gives it away.

"The man in the car," she says.

He nods, pleased in spite of himself. He toes up to the lawn to extend a hand. Her own hand disappears in his, but her grip shakes him. "I live in the yellow house." He points over his shoulder. He tells her his name, says, "Call me Pinky," and he wants to say, *All my friends do,* but thinks, *What friends?* and feels a surge of despair. What folly. What gall. What enormous odds. It's overwhelming, this business of love.

"Pinky," her voice rises. "Rose. I'm Rose Spencer." She doesn't release his fingertips, instead stalks up the lawn with Pinky in tow. "Tell me, what this is?" Rose disengages her hand to point at a branch. In the upper reaches there is a cocoon, a tented web, with freckled bits splotted here and there. In yet another branch, he sees the start of another, and how is it that he hasn't noticed them before? He sights down the row of cottonwoods streetside, the upper reaches. He sighs.

"Tent caterpillars," he says. He hopes she doesn't register the way his flesh quivers as he thinks of the frantic shivering of worms overhead. A phobia, like some folks have for snakes, spiders.

"Are they bad? For the tree?" she asks.

He knows they'll eat their way down a branch, mature, and drop like fruit. He backs up a pace. No more than a couple tents. Not so bad. "We'll keep an eye on them." And suddenly he's using "we," and such audacity stuns him. But she lets him get away with it, nodding her head and escorting him off her lawn.

"If you need anything," he says. "I have a car," he says, "for groceries, anything." She's watching, and he has the sense she's backing away, though her feet are still rooted to the edge of the lawn. "I'm safe," he says, ducks his head.

"How's that?" she asks.

He flushes. Can't believe he's saying this. "Well, you can probably run faster than I can." He laughs as he's always had to.

Rose arches an eyebrow at him. "I don't know what you expect from me." She crosses her arms, cups an elbow in each palm. "But

I'm tapped out when it comes to men. Pity, love, anger, compassion—you name it, and I've exhausted it."

"I'm sorry," Pinky says, and he means it. He wonders what could have hurt her so deeply, briefly envies her pain, the experience of being close enough to wound or be wounded. And then, of course, he realizes that's nonsense. Believes he has the perfect vantage for sympathy, from behind this great bulwark of flesh. He's thinking of himself now—the lifetime alone, avoiding pain. He runs a hand down his chest, down the globe of his belly, a gesture he's developed over the years familiarizing himself with the expanding boundaries of his body. "We're neighbors," he says, and she seems puzzled, but there's something in his face, or his tone, that puts her at ease.

She relaxes the grip on her arms, and says, "Neighbors. I can handle that."

It's his turn to be confused now. He checks his watch, then looks west, to the sunset, as though that might be more accurate. "I have to get on to work—over at the school? I'm the maintenance technician." A smile sweeps across his face. "Night janitor." He avoids her eyes, looks over her shoulder, and the hills rising above the town turn amber, then the color of autumn rushes and where the light catches the grasses, the bunched sage, it is a luminous fire. It occurs to him just how long it's been since he's *seen* the hills, wonders how it is that he could have moved through these days, these months without noticing how the crowns levitate with light above the rim rock, the dimming crevasses. He backs up a step, and as she turns her attention once again on the yard, he starts away, first one foot and then the other until he finds himself three blocks gone and on the steps of school. He unlocks the door with a jangle of keys, lets them loose to the satisfying snatch and click of the take-up reel, then enters the building. He clamps the door shut, and, flipping on hall lights, he breaks into his best Johnny Mathis voice, *"Chances are..."*

They shop together now. One day a week. Separate carts. He's taken it upon himself to keep Rose advised on lawn maintenance. "It's the first yard I've ever taken care of," she confides, and so he understands she's always had a man, and no, he won't infringe because it's obvious she takes delight in adding oil to the lawn mower gasoline, or pruning the boxwood hedges, regards each task as an indication of competence in the larger world. "I believe a person could fix anything," she says in the house utensils aisle, "given proper instruction and duct tape." Then she adds, "Except trust." And this is the first hint she's given of what keeps her so clearly focused on staying "neighborly."

Not that he's done much more than buddy his grocery cart up to hers, and although it's true, the contents have more and more begun to resemble hers, still he keeps a cautious distance. He's at a standstill, and all the month of long hours mulled over the mop handle at work, dreaming up ways to woo and win her, have yielded nothing more than any neighbor could claim.

Until today, when she lets slip the tidbit about trust. And then the store manager, Ray Tipp, an old classmate—a starved-looking man who keeps himself anxious with coffee—checks out Pinky's groceries, says, "Got a sale on Hostess Ho-Ho's." He lifts a head of broccoli and Roman Meal bread. "You on a diet?"

Pinky can't even run. He feels Rose, next in line, caught up in his embarrassment. He shuffles between the checkout stands, the backside of his trousers snag on a magazine rack, and he endures Ray's curiosity while he frees himself without spilling *Vogue* and *Look* into the aisle. He pays Ray, lifts his bagged groceries from the grinning stock boy. He knows that this, too, Rose must see, how the young boy's eyes widen and the whites shine like twin moons, roll in their sockets.

Stupid. Stupid to have invited her along. To see this. Still stupid—after all these years—to aim yourself at inevitable hurt. But the damage is done. Rose, after all, is guilty by association, and so he pivots on his heel, the great slowing mass of him, to face this small woman and take her disgust in stride.

She's handing money to Ray. Two twenties, a ten. She fishes out a single and another. Some change. She takes her bags from the boy and waits for Pinky to lead the way, which he does with all the grace he can muster. When he breaks out into the sunshine, his heart is cluttering his chest, so huge, so full it's become. He puffs crossing the parking lot, the bags swinging at his sides, and he sets them on the ground to open the car door for her.

Two blocks from the store, she says, "Why don't you pull into the park? I've bought a melon. We can have a bite."

Just like that.

And why not? he thinks. A picnic, something he hasn't done since his mother passed on, and for a brief moment he can almost hear her, see the woman she was, all comfort—bosomy and dimpled elbows—pressing food onto him, the sound of other children chasing and laughing. He is hiccuping tears. "Eat," she says. "Like a good boy. Never mind those others. They're jealous you gotta momma can cook." She chucks a finger under his chin. "Your daddy was a *big* man." By this he understands that he, too, would be ... large ... and in her eyes that was good.

Rose directs him onto River Street and down to the small riverside park. He used to come here as a younger man, walked the levy at night to imagine himself with a woman, strolling the paths or swooning on a bench in the grip of passion and the moony night, like any one of a number of couples whispering from behind the willows' curtains, or lolling in the tall, blue grasses riverside.

He follows Rose's lead, carrying the plastic-sacked melon in both hands like a gift, an offering of the magi, and she brings them to the base of a cottonwood. He is breaking a sweat, and the air is brilliant with light on water so that he squints the moisture from his eyes, releases a great round sigh, "Aaah," and he's just so damned grateful for these simple pleasures—river, melon, woman—that he's unlikely to recover his voice any time soon so he sighs again.

Rose has seated herself in the grass. He wishes she were wearing a flowing skirt, frilly blouse, a wide-brimmed straw hat, instead of the baggy jeans and T-shirt that slouch on her tiny frame, and then he feels an ingrate. Clothes. What do they signify? Certainly not the moment. She takes the melon from him, plops it in her lap like a placid child, then pats the grass beside her, and he faces the task of lowering himself. Pinky thinks to remain standing, strike a noble pose, but she's already gazing off across the wide, blue river to the hills opposite. He braces one hand against the tree, crooks a knee, stretches the other leg behind, and bends cautiously forward and down and down some more. It's a struggle against mass, gravity. His joints pop in series. He tries not to gasp or puff, and that's nearly as much effort as kneeling. His crotch feels like a wishbone, ready to snap, and then he's down without having fallen. His face is red; he can tell. He filches a handkerchief out of his rear pocket and towels off his forehead, neck, the skinny V of flesh between the unbuttoned top of his button-up shirt.

"Do you have a knife?" she asks.

And he does, though he must lean back, lift his stomach, and squeeze his hand in the narrow flap of cloth, cutting the blood to his fingers as he feels for the knife. Finally, he frees it, a pocket Buck knife with all the appointments—even a corkscrew. But she lifts the knife away, slaps the screw back into its steel nest, and locks open the large blade. She stabs into the melon's meat, saws a chunk free, and scrapes the seeds back into the exposed heart of the fruit. She hands the wedge to him, and he waits for her to join him.

"People on the whole are an unlikable bunch," she says, sinks the knife to the hilt into the melon's rind. "Take my advice. Never fall in love with them."

Pinky laughs, but it's a squeezed little thing, his chest constricting.

"You think you know cruelty, I know you do." She saws into the melon. "But the cruelty of strangers, or friends, is nothing," she wags a finger in his face, "compared to what love can do." She is tightlipped. Her brows beetle, and the air about her seems charged with a static energy. She bites into the melon, tells him about her first husband, his one-night stands, moves on to her second husband and his affairs. Tells it all in four short sentences, as if she can't bite off the ends of words hard enough, spit it out fast enough.

"What did I learn from it, you want to know..."

She dabbles at the corner of her mouth with a fingertip, where some melon juice drips down, and Pinky thinks he has never seen anything more delectable. He'd like to take her finger into his mouth and suck it dry.

She stretches her legs out, leans against the tree, and tells him of her third and last husband's affairs. How she then called the woman, wanted to see her. "Couldn't help myself. Called a complete stranger—though it seemed I had the right, we'd shared so much. I don't know what I expected. She came to my house. Not the first time, I could tell that right off—the way she found her way to his chair."

Rose rubbed the back of her head against the tree's bark, a leisurely scratching. "She was a short, stumpy-legged little thing, not cute, no, not even handsome. But interesting. Perky. She says, 'I didn't mean to ruin your life.' She was being sincere, but of course, she was flattering herself. After all, my life wasn't ruined. Merely changed. I told her that."

She looked over at Pinky. "Don't you wonder at how I could be so collected? So smug?"

"I can't imagine," Pinky says.

"No." She leans over, pats his hand. "Of course you can't. And of course, I was full of crap." She sighed. "If my life wasn't ruined, it was the next thing to it. Rubble. That's what I was left with. Rubble."

She squeezes her left breast, and Pinky knows it is her heart she means, but all he can picture is the tender flesh crumpled in her fist, and he wants to loosen her fingers, cradle her breast and heart in the palm of his hand, which he discovers is sweating so he swipes it down his pant leg. And then, wonder of all wonders, he reaches over with his newly dried hand and takes the melon from her, lifts the knife away, slices another piece, skins and offers it to her.

Which she declines.

"Three strikes, you're out. Isn't that right?" she asks.

"In baseball," Pinky says, and he wants to sound decisive, but hears how his voice trails off. He's stuck with the melon wedge, dripping through his fingers onto his pant leg.

"Yes," she agrees. "In baseball *and in men.*"

And what can Pinky say? He eats the melon slice, wipes his hand on the grass. On the river, a pair of Canada geese paddle upstream, six goslings drafting in their wake. Sunlight crooks across the water's surface, and shadows swim the face of the hills opposite. Pinky blinks, feels moisture budding behind his eyes, and blinks again. He begins to comprehend the scale of his task— wooing this woman—even if he weren't hobbled by his own body. He's still holding the knife, and he looks down at his belly, wishes he could slice away the flesh, pare down to some more supple version of himself that would be capable of the acrobatics—walking, sitting, bending over—that normal, everyday people perform in everyday courtship. He wants to be handsome for her.

A pair of young girls roller-blade down the sidewalk, the wheels buzzing with the sound of enormous hummingbirds. They wind down the path, skinny legs and arms knotted in protective pads. Their laughter is a shouting, and Pinky admires the honesty of it. He wonders what Rose sounds like when she laughs. He wonders if she laughs.

Rubble, she'd said, and he questions the state her heart's in now. "I'm not like those men," he says.

"Why?" she asks. "Because you're fat?" And it's just a statement. "Because you think other women wouldn't find you attractive?"

Truth is he hadn't thought of it that way, but he begins to see this could work for him. He nods.

"Another way that you're safe?" she asks.

He nods again, though he feels like he's stepping into something unseen, something with teeth.

She stares across the river. "Do you think that little of yourself, or me?"

It's worse than he'd feared, certain now that she despises him for his clumsiness, his transparent eagerness. He blames himself and his lack of experience; he blames the hour of the day and the bristling grass that torments his ankles. He tells her he's a fool and that he respects her and her friendship. Those are the words he uses, *respect* and *friendship,* and she continues to stare out across the river. He asks her to understand, he's not used to … to … picnics.

Her brows furrow, and she says, as if she hasn't heard him, "My last husband was different. Where the others'd been tall, he was short. A bookish man with a sense of humor. He couldn't change the oil in the car, but he was mad for opera. I believed he was different, as day is to night." She wags her head. "But finally, he was only a different kind of night. And this is much too lovely a day," she leans back on her elbows, "to quibble. I'm done with men." Rose rolls onto her side, facing Pinky. "Except as friends. Take it or leave it."

Pinky nods and heaves a sigh, but even as she pats his hand and closes her eyes to rest, he is studying the logistics of getting back on his feet.

Late at night, in the gym, Pinky plots strategy. He turns on the overheads, and the constellation of bulbs shine from the floor's mirror finish. He has cleaning down to an art, dry-mopping the area in under an hour, starting at the foot of the bleachers, left to right, and threading his way in overlapping lanes down and back until he's dusted his way into the boys' locker room, where the real work begins. Though, as it is summer, this chore is reduced to a twice weekly touchup instead of the nightly tour during the school year. He switches to a wet mop, fills the big steel bucket on casters with hot water, a splash of disinfectant Sparkle and bleach. He works backwards, kicking the bucket ahead of him like a troublesome dog. The mop bangs against lockers, and Pinky loves the rat-a-tat-tat off the empty doors. Sings "Frankie and Johnnie" to their machine-gun accompaniment. Sees himself as Johnnie, but can't imagine doing her wrong, can't conceive of such discontent. He rolls the bucket into the boys' bathroom. Lifts his voice to the tiled walls. *At least that's the way the story goes. Frankie bought everything for Johnnie, from his sports car to his Ivy League clothes.* He buffs the floor, glances in the mirror.

His face seems different, and maybe it's just love has transformed him. Or has he lost weight? He lifts the putty knife from the cart, scrapes at a wad of paper toweling glommed to the underside of a sink. When he straightens up, he fidgets a finger into his waistband, snugs in two. Yes. Oh yes. He's lost weight. *Friend came running to Frankie, said, You know I wouldn't tell you no lie. I saw your man driving that sports car with a chick named Nellie Bligh—*

And this is the tough part. He enters a stall. How can he convince Rose of his own true heart? And damn it. He slaps the brush in the toilet bowl, squirts in blue disinfectant, swabs, and flushes. He deserves one good shot at it, doesn't he? He slaps the cover up, scrubs—cover down—scrubs—backs out of the stall, then moves on to the next and the next. Patience, he tells himself, and though he's only known Rose as a friend and neighbor a little over two months, he's got a forty-year backlog of empty nights, and Pinky stops, envisions the calamity of another forty empty years, and finds himself doubled over one of the toilets. When his heart calms in his chest and the angina eases under his left wing bone, he backs out of the stall. The room is bright, as only locker-room bathrooms can be with the high banks of fluorescent lights buzzing and reflecting off the mirrors and stainless steel doors, the white, porcelain sinks and urinals all ablaze so that when he looks in the mirror this time what he sees is his forehead shining with sweat and the enormous bell of his body overexposed in white overalls, and for a moment he loses himself against the white wall tiles.

He leaves the bucket and mop, the toilet brush and disinfectant, and crosses back through the locker room, turning off lights as he goes, through the gym and out the side door. He stands on the asphalt stoop. In the school parking lot, the arc lamp's cone of light seethes with winged insects—swirling, bumping, a luminous feast that the nighthawks scoop through. Pinky breathes deeply, feels the moist back of his shirt cooling. Crickets pick up where they'd left off. He steps away from the building and walks until the locked school folds into the night. He walks slow and steady, his heart easing, chest lightening. He knows he will have to return to work, but for now he turns up a side street where lamplight streams out onto porches and grass.

He stays to the sidewalk, but glances in each house. Where drapes are open, it's the furniture he notices—which place has a piano, or a lamp centered in the window like a beacon. Then there are all the dining rooms with tables bunkered by chairs. So many chairs. Seascapes over the sofa, mounted deer, or the grouping of family pictures like a lineup in the post office. Once in a while he glimpses the people. Sometimes he believes he can smell their dinner: chicken, hamburger, barbeque ribs. Or more vaguely Italian cuisine, Oriental, Middle East. He feels a stirring of hunger, but he tucks his two fingers into his waistband again and thinks apple instead of apple pie. He journeys down another side street and exchanges greetings with a man smoking a pipe on his front porch. He passes a young couple, and the woman titters, but they don't notice Pinky, so wrapped up are they, and he finds that utterly disarming. He meets more people strolling under the streetlamps. Why, it seems to him, that the whole town must be spilling out into the warm night. Or maybe this is the way the world congregates when he's alone, in his school, his home. And there it is. His house. Locked tight and shuttered close. He opens the front door, the drapes, turns on all the lights. Then he steps back out on the sidewalk to see what he can of himself. He's reluctant to look, but discovers he doesn't fare so badly. Tomorrow, first thing, he will dig out the old photos, frame the one of his mother and father's wedding, the portrait of his grandfather—big-chested, with thighs like a Percheron. It will take so little, he thinks, and he pivots on his heel to look across the street, to the house of his beloved. The lights behind the drapes are a wan glow, and he's stricken with how tidy the place is, how self-contained. He feels . . . what is it? Not exactly love, but a stirring that is equally unfamiliar from his end of things, and . . . disconcerting—call it pity. He wishes he could step into her life as easily as his home, open it wide to this sweet night. He heaves a sigh, and looks up, over the trees and over the tops of houses to where the distant hills shoulder the dark beneath the quickening stars.

He means to take her on a date, but he doesn't call it that. He doesn't dare. He mentions the movie, casually, over groceries. He tells Rose, "Dutch treat," to allay her suspicion. It's a love story, but he doesn't mention that, either. She offers to buy the popcorn. "Only fair," she says. "All the gas you've used on grocery trips."

Pinky accepts. He feels pretty smart. Of course he hasn't thought about the theater seats, and though his pants are looser now and sitting upright no longer cuts off his wind, still it's a tight, tight squeeze, but he manages. He's appreciative for her small kindness of unbuttered popcorn. She'd noticed his weight loss a couple days ago. "Hope you're not doing this for me," she'd said, and when he replied, "No," he could see she was unprepared for the truth, some small part of her stung by his admission. He felt encouraged.

It *was* a sappy film. Any other time he would have been the first to ridicule the sentimentality. Except, now it is Rose scoffing, and that provokes in him a desire to defend it. She curls her lip, and Pinky lets his heart go soft. Walking back to the car, she recaps some of the *lowlights*. When she snorts at the dialogue, Pinky taps her arm with a finger, says, "You could give it a chance."

"You can't mean it."

"It had heart," he says.

She pinches his arm. "It had a lobotomy. Not the same thing."

"Ouch," he says.

She goes on, "What you don't know," she shakes a finger at him, "is this kind of willful ignorance about the *realities* of love wearies me sometimes."

They drive away from the theater in silence. He wants to talk, but is embarrassed to admit that there's little willful about his ignorance. Inexperience, certainly.

He suggests the 410 Drive In for a bite, and she agrees. Rose's hamburger fills her hands, drapes over fingers, lobs chunks of lettuce and pickle into the napkin covering her lap while Pinky's grilled chicken breast sandwich is a pale, insignificant thing in comparison. It hardly seems worth the effort. He takes baby bites to stretch it out. She offers him a sip of her malt, and it's so intimate a gesture he's dumbfounded. He accepts the plastic cup from her hands and takes the straw—squeezed between her lips just moments earlier—into his mouth, tongues the tip tenderly. It is a jolt of pure chocolate, cold and clean and sweet. His eyes close.

So this is what it's like—the taste of a woman, and there's a curious quivering at the base of his spine. And of course he *knows* that's not the case, but he enjoys the *idea* of it and has to stop himself from draining her malt.

"You think I'm harsh," she says, "about the movie. But the point is," she crumples the emptied hamburger wrapping, "romantic love suggests we are incomplete without another, in need of salvation. You're led to believe that you'll be a better person if there's someone around to expect it. But somewhere down the line, you find the cost of these expectations too dear. What? you say. Eat the same cooking? Sleep on the same side of the bed? Give up variety? Implausible if not impossible. All you will *ask* for is a little kindness, but what you will *want* is more than anybody can give—their undivided attention for the rest of their life—and so you struggle and struggle and hurt each other endlessly.

"Three marriages, over twenty-five years' worth. Imagine— twenty-five years attempting love. Trust me. It's a complication you're better off without."

Rose sighs, pats her lips dry, then sets the soiled napkin and empty malt cup back on the serving tray. "Take me home," she says. She sounds utterly weary.

Pinky takes a deep breath, resettles in the seat. His stomach bumps the steering wheel. He drives the long way, down Bridge Street, over to Riverside, up to Highland, slowly. How painful she makes it sound, *twenty-five years,* but all he can think of is turning over in bed to find someone there, of eating someone else's cooking, and it sounds grand to Pinky, worth the risk, the heartache. He *knows* what it's like to be alone—the long haul of it, not the early phase, when the day winds down because *you've* nothing better to do and stretching across an empty bed still seems a luxury.

It's coming onto seven in the evening, and the sky is yet bright with daylight. He stops at the school, invites her in. He shows her the broom closet, the mops. He shows her classrooms, the new computer lab—shakes his head, feather dusting, he explains. He takes her into the gym, throws on the lights just to show her how the floor shines. He stands center court and lobs a high A at her. He could almost swear she blushes. He proceeds to sing the only song he can think of with her name in the title, "The Yellow Rose of Texas."

On the way out of the building, she says, "A most unlikely, but lovely serenade. Thank you." They leave the car there to walk the three blocks home. He knows she slows her pace to match his. It is early evening, and the shortening daylight lapses into a dim gloaming. Dusky-winged ash aphids are swarming—bumbling clouds of blue-bodied mites that rise like yeast from the grass. Late summer, they come down from the Camas and Palouse Prairies to swim in the warmer valley air. By full evening, they will web together in gray winding sheets around the south side of the ash tree trunks, where they will shiver into their final, short-lived ecstasy. But now they are a squall, riding the turmoil of heat convections and cooling drafts. They speckle the couple's clothes, dust their hair. Pinky is enthralled with the tiny creatures, the enormous bulb of their bodies and improbable flight. They bobble and fall, rise and fumble. This is not a matter of grace.

Rose waves a hand through the air in front of her. They stop on the far edge of the cloud, and Rose ducks her head, swipes at an eye. Pinky can see a bead of aphids riding her eyelashes.

"Ow," she says, her eye tearing.

"Here," he comforts, nips her chin between thumb and forefinger, lifts her face to what is left of the light. Rose is a woman who has little truck with makeup. There's no attempt to disguise the lines, the thinning skin. He is captivated, as he was the first time he saw her, by the static energy of this woman, her relentless honesty, all her life available in her face, her eyes. And this is the thing he both fears and admires, how she has been pared down to the bone, tried and fired as he never has been. Though his fingers barely grace her chin, he feels her energy, some galvanic current of old doubts running through her, and she sidesteps under his hand. He takes a steadying breath, says, "Hold still." He spits on his free thumb, touches that small drop of moisture to the corner of her eye. The speck of blue floats off the white, onto Pinky's thumb, and he neatly lifts it away.

Up and down the block, house lights come on, and children shoo cats out of front doors. The hills over the town flatten, grow larger with the dark. There's no help for it, but Pinky feels a melancholy he's hard put to explain, and it has to do with the onset of dark and the sudden still. It has to do with the small woman at his side, her mistrust, and his own lifetime of hiding, in his house, his work, and foremost his own flesh. And, he sees it has to do with fear—the way we run through our lives in terror of it—and everything to do with despair, and perhaps, he thinks, that is what despair is, finally, a lack of daring. He feels savvy. Overhead, a crow lifts from the treetop, banks toward the river with a hard laugh—ha, ha, ha.

In another block they stop again so that Pinky can catch his breath. He pants in the quiet, shakes his head. He will lose weight—he will because he cannot go on as he always has, he understands this now—but he also knows he will always be big. Not small, or even trim, and he is struck by this. It has been with him so long, this ocean of flesh. Pinky feels he must tell Rose. Warn her. "I will always be fat," he says.

"Yes," she agrees. She lays a hand on his forearm. "As I will always be bitter," she says.

They stand that way in the new dark, and he thinks, should a young husband look out from his living room window, or should the young wife hurrying home from errands come across them standing so, they would think Rose and Pinky some middle-aged couple of long years—the way Rose's hand is anchored on his arm. And he wonders about the couples he has so long envied, how much is illusion—a public face for the private griefs and hurts they harbor? He thinks of the depth of Rose's bitterness, the earnest way in which she confirms it, and he understands it's as deep and abiding as the bones seated in the continent of his flesh. It humbles him, how fiercely she is grounded in her resolve.

And he does not feel up to the task. Sees himself as the lightweight in this struggle. His stomach gripes, and will not be consoled by the pat of his hand. How he already misses the easy comfort of food, the anonymity. He feels a nervousness, an anxiousness like a missed meal, or the temptation of chocolate before sleep. He sways from foot to foot, rocking in place. A terror steals upon him that he cannot fathom, so that his feet are seized in place and his fat plumbs him to the earth while she stands stark and quiet at his side as if forged of consequences larger than his imagining. He sees she is not the rod, but the lightning itself, flinty bits striking off—old loves, grudges, misfortunes, a hundred errors in judgment and more—quizzing his friable heart. He should run. He should bolt, for he senses this is a struggle deeper than the naïve courtship he'd embarked on. Not the territory of novices. Not for the uninitiated. It is a journey of days, years, a chronic case of heartache, the relentless wooing to win and lose, again and again. He almost laughs, for all his assurances to Rose of how safe he is—he sees now that it is *she* who is the danger... always has been.

Overhead, the clouds quail beneath the rising moon. He turns his face away. He slows his panic by imagining the imaginable: the march of days, the orderliness of work—nights, cleaning, trips to the grocery store, lawn care, and diets. Conversation that spills over from day to day, and running jokes. He wonders how they will look in a year, two, five. Will she grow generous as he grows slight? He steadies, takes a deep breath. What he wants, he realizes, more than anything, is to imagine a time when fear will carry no weight in his heart. When love will need no proof. He squints into the dark, as if to make out the features of that distant time—the heel of a foot striking the floor as she steps down from her side of his bed, the shape of her face, is it Rose? But he cannot know this. Not now. Not yet. And, perhaps, for now, the question is enough. He quashes the impulse to push back his sleeves. Instead, he leads them arm in arm, their bodies swaying each its own way, beneath the steepled canopy of sycamore where the first flush of moonrise swims the wavering shadows in a school of light.

The Mattress

Meredith Drum is an atomic bomb, a puppet, is confetti and napalm.

Maybe she's a peony grown annually for the flower show. This year's first-prize installation, a Hiroshima Imperial Hotel room shattered, bouquets wetting the beds.

Through the woods, in darkness obscuring our feet, she leads a few thieves. Foxfire on the trees. She rubs the phosphors on our faces.

Young gods are seduced: she brings them coffee laced with fixative. Snaking down her street, tongues darting, they hide behind rats and trash cans.

In city parks, you are fatted and sedate from being served, she might be waiting under bridges for your riches. No worry, she won't hear you.

The officials call her plagiarist. They tie her to the ladder to the roof, and at her feet they burn her books. One of Tomaz Salamun's receives her final look.

Meredith Drum is quiet at night and in the day; she will never be silenced.

In Charm School she was blindfolded, left in a Rhododendron Maze. In record time, she appeared at the exit, arms scratched and bleeding.

Her neighbor kneels by her sleeping head, the wall between, recording the sounds that fall from her tongue. If the wall disappeared their heads would meet.

The beach is empty in winter, except for a few Russians.
Meredith Drum walks in the water: the shooting galleries are
closed, the aquarium and Ferris wheel closed. The roller coaster
blackened, a bird aviary in summer. Terns and gulls aren't
nesting.

One of her hands is weaker than the other (we are lucky). Their
likeness should be cast in bronze, sculpted bigger than any man,
placed in the traffic circle below the Pulaski Skyway.

Meredith Drum knows of a mattress under the bridge that
people dream on. They say they have never slept there.

Too much money in her pockets will be taken on the way home.
The hand keeps reaching in, finding more, leaving grime on
thumbed lips, a clean taste like metal on the back of teeth.

Her audience is fooled into thinking she's good-looking; they
pull at her clothes and search their faces in the mirror. But she's
growing old. Her body's cavities collapsing even now.

Meredith Drum sits in a room talking to someone sitting in a
room but in the South Pacific. Ham radios rusted from
condensation.

If burned as tallow she might light Shea Stadium for the season.

The Hotel Delano

At the Delano, the flags are flying half-mast,
Honoring the workers released from debt and poverty
By the death of parents, by murder, freed by inheritance.

"We've killed them all," shout the street cleaners
Marching through the lobby with bloodstained hands.
Chambermaids wrap themselves like brides in the damask drapes,

"We poisoned ours, their miserly selves, their money
Better spent now than saved for their useless age."
The cabby smokes a cigar, lounges on the fainting couch,

Ran his father over, the loaded codger caught in the road.
Cabby's a made-man, a dent on his bumper his only remorse.
The cooks dance on the billiards table, the bellhop swings

From lamps. The rich peer over the balcony in fear
Or huddle in guestrooms calculating the fortunes
Lost when the debt of the poor is cleared.

Poolside over my grandmother's body, I'd held her under
Until she stilled. From her mouth I'm pulling a colored rope
Of handkerchiefs tied together, they rise through her throat.

Hands

Sleeping in your Harlem apartment,
I lie on the bed by the window to the airshaft,
a dark flume cutting the center of the building,
a pigeon's alley from basement to roof.
My head on the sill, I stretch my hands out.

You're in the next room at the upright,
winning a young composer's prize.
I don't hear. I don't hear
your fingers' discipline,
their ache and practiced
loss of everything else.

I'm out climbing the airshaft,
pressing words in the mortar cracks,
hurling my body onto the black tar roof,
mumbling in rhyme as I leap the firewalls,
ambition heavy on the horizon.

I'm receptive as a trout
when you find me,
and lay your hands on,
in the places where disappointment hides,
measuring faith
between my thighs.
But you are giving me hands
the piano already owns.

Civic Remedy Almanac

I. *Frigg's Linchpin*

Vinyl spinning, midnight pimping in Mick's gin mill, my lips
mining this fish fry, till my thigh minx Iris flits hips with Jimmy.
His pigmy mind thinking I'm blind, thinking bilk, grinding his
milt digit with Iris's fig. I'll chill his smirk, slit his midriff. My
fist's flying, his spit's flinging. I'm hissing. I'm lit within.
Skirmish this picknick. Vim.

II. *Hex Length*

Between these green creek beds by the seven cypresses, we've
seen beetles screw. Wedged between egg nests, felled trees, red
lecterns, we emerged, pressed the ledger, my debt, between her
legs, left. Tell me when her welts mend, her checks reddened,
we'll send fey by needled letter, kestrel the hennery, reenter my
temptress dress. She'll tremble. We've shred.

III. *Ballad Atalanta*

A fact, Atalanta ran track fast, spat at lads that grasp Samsara.
What a sassy gal; asks why marry? Sadly, Dad wants a cash czar,
has a tacky palm. Atalanta allays Pa's plan. Any bach that can
pass a vamp's fast arm, catch's a vamp's hand. Alas, a dandy, all
yang, plays Galahad's balls at Atalanta's track. An asphalt crash. A
smash, a flash, all's awry. A Brahma zaps Atalanta away, a gypsy
cab's madcap path. Away all masks. Away Maya. Dada. Thanks.

Mail-Order Chameleon

Sent for by mail, a chameleon waits
with the rest of the freight
for a name. Our name.

We risk fraud for what
arrives in 8–10 weeks: a limp form,
silent at first, but alive.

Guaranteed it will improve,
we allow for quiet,
for its remove in the terrarium:

haven't we summoned nature
to our door, enjoyed
life's measure in miniature?

We'll all adapt. We'll play records,
the radio, watch TV, even talk
to ourselves. Meanwhile it will listen—

Meanwhile, the night will let down
her mane of hair in all directions.
The chameleon will never sleep.

Men come, posse after posse,
and still no cry. As for us,
what voice remains seldom behaves. We swear

that as customers, we deserve to discover
how the pet arrives in its own
color-shifting skin. We'll order another.

Who among us will say to the postman
that it was born wrong
with its versatile foot-long tongue?

Wit's End

My father says, "Face it, you live
   in a civilization of mirrors and sinks,"
     invading my real room, the bathroom.

I pull down an eyelid till I see the pained
   pink meniscus underneath. I "O"
     my mouth, poke the mascara wand

at my eyelashes, not missing
   by much. It's makeup's premonition
     of sex in the house he can't stand.

The bathroom's littered with eyeliners,
   tweezers, kisslipped tissues. I shed snarls
     of hair in the shower like saffron threads,

red kelp. In the mirror I paint myself a clownface
   copied from *Sassy, Seventeen, Glamour.* He
     stands in the doorway, loving

the used-to-be lovable 12-year-old
   formerly his. We look in the mirror:
     blush welts, orange, riding low

on my cheeks, pink lipstick leaking
   from my lip corners. Glitter-white
     chevrons for eyelids; Cover Girl fails

again to cover my nose-zits. Reflected, behind me,
   tangles of the unwashed bras I don't need
     trail from shower rod, shampoo rack,

hot-cold dial, soapdish, stopcock.
    He hates it: me mooning, me sighing,
        me incessantly hairbrushing, singing stupid

love songs. "I'll buy back the gunk!" he says.
    He'll pay twice what I spent if only I'll stop.
        I stand by the tub in the bathroom,

my real room. I prop up a leg, I pull up
    my skirt, start shaving thigh-stubble. I shove
        the door shut between us with my ass.

Highlights

Drunk, her eyes would water and sparkle
and she'd hold my jaw in her palm
as though I were her child or dog, saying,
*Listen to me, Douglas. Don't dare turn
into one of these aging bachelor teachers.*
Then she'd reel off names of half a dozen
doddering men in the physics and social
studies departments who wandered the halls
in stained shirts and chalked-up pants
frayed at the pockets, men first in line
every day in the faculty cafeteria,
men who stared deadpan into the lens
of the yearbook photographer.

Come with me, she said. We took a cab
to her gay guy in the Village. She said
I needed once and for all a decent
haircut. She was first. Barry
put a tight rubber cap on her head
and used a hooked needle to pull
strands of her wet hair through holes
until she looked like a shock therapy patient,
her face pale and tired in the light,
and suddenly she was a woman
twenty years older than me getting
highlights. Though she looked damn
good when it was over, climbing
down from the chair in her red shoes.
We found a bar on Bleecker Street.
She put a hand through my new haircut
while I complained about the girls in American
Literature who were giving me problems.
She said they were in love with me,

and wondered at how blind I was
to miss it. Then she told me, finally,
where she went every weekend: Tampa,
to stay with an auto parts salesman
who paid her fare. A man her age, a man
who used to be married to her sister.

Crossing Over

Just as, a stand of trees before you—
you now sit turned sideways, on a trail rock,
incidentally, listening to see what comes
up, down, or out, if you do manage
to contain your clumsy sighs, your leafy
rustles—to pass the time you idly
eye up one far pine to where a birch
crosses it, then follow that
as you follow wavewash crisscross
at the shore—those long surf-fingers
unclenched nearly to separatedness,
really, for only 20 or 30 heartbeats
(as though ocean and moon hadn't argued
over their precious course for aeons,
scoring them out on the shores of Bali,
Singapore, Tarentum,
Scamander, and Ararat)
before relapsing to the common—
and the canopy beneath the arch
their crisscross makes is light green, pellucid,
so, as you walk home, past the August
corn, night has already set
in those even fields too thickly sown
for you to cross, and a humble cricket-song
is rising to you from the hump-grass at its edge.

How to Leave a Small Town Like Yours

The third time we made love
the magic was already gone.
We should have stopped right
there, but instead we moved
into an apartment, adopted
a cat you named Pharaoh,
and took a long car trip
to the mountains. By then
the circus was in town.
A handful of tough-looking
dwarves in black leather
drank at the Wagon Wheel
that weekend. "Just try and toss
us," the tall one kept saying,
"just try." Your mother came
to visit and we ate funnel cake
among interesting strangers.
It was like the last supper.
Bloodlines showed,
and I could see you in thirty years.
Not bad. But I wasn't happy,
Pharaoh always stoned
on catnip. The little people
leaving on Monday,
and your mother would stay,
so I kissed you both
on my way to bed, slipped
out at dawn with the cat,
and took only that paper bag
of ripe figs from the kitchen table.

Curse Two: The Naming

Katherine, Katherine, Katherine, Katherine.
Black hair, small cold eyes, whom you loved.
Cocktease Katherine, chewer of souls.
The door blew open and she blew in, a ghoul.
Black air, small cold wind, taking everything.
Fish-eater Katherine, whose nails dig blood.
I'm going to call her pinch-cunt, pickle-lip
piss-dribble, shit-smear, goat's-meat breath.
I want to throw stones at her mother's corpse,
send her children to name-change foster homes.
May the coat she is wearing burst into flames
and boil the flesh blistering off her bones.
May she be refused in both heaven and hell
and wander the earth forever without rest,
a hungry ghost clinging to the rocks and trees.

The Errand

At my father's request I went into the city
to ask for the Senator's daughter's hand.
But she said she would not have me, nor any man.
It was, I thought, a great pity:

she was not only wealthy, but very pretty.

So I told her that I would stand
on the spot of earth where I'd been rejected
and each night she would hear my demand
until she recanted, and accepted.

For three nights I shivered as the constellations
wheeled about my head, and I repeated my offer.
Finally, on the third night, her father
put his arm around me and brought me to the kitchen.
We drank scotch. He told me she would not change her decision.
He gave me his second daughter as a consolation.

Trout Quintet

1.

Where water meets water,
where rain hangs lead-heavy for days
before finally deciding to harden and fall,
where the nearest road is sixty miles away
and that a narrow track of gravel,
where the lake is as still as a photograph
and has never been photographed,
where the trout return in accordance with a schedule
that is not a human schedule,
following a water-ridden brain-map,
a hardwired river route, an instinct chart,

Tom Thomson sits in a canoe playing solitaire.
Each time he loses,
he throws his cards into the water.
Each time he wins
he catches a trout.

2.

He likes this place
because the satellites cannot see it
and the water is pure.
He likes this place
because it is where the trout come,
where they stop.
He likes this place
because parsley and wild tomatoes
grow naturally on the banks.
He likes the way
his canoe fits the water.
He likes the way
the water fits the earth.

Is Tom Thomson a figure of legend?
Tom Thomson is a living totem pole.
Is Tom Thomson larger than life?
Four men could stand in Tom Thomson's shadow,
smoking cigars and talking about baseball.

One night four men came for him
carrying official papers and sawed-off shotguns.
A week later their Chevy Suburban was found.
The motor was running. The left turn indicator blinking.
The glove box was filled with trout.

3.
"There is much joy to be found
in the imprecise usage of words."
Tom Thomson disagrees. He slams his bottle
down on the wooden table. The wood,
anticipating the bottle's arrival,
splinters in advance.

Who would call a trout a salmon?
But words are arbitrary.
Who would call a trout an iceberg?
Call it what you want, it will not come.

Tom Thomson's grunt clears the forest of birds.
His laughter frightens the gods.
The philosopher Pythagoras devised a method
of measuring Tom Thomson by taking the length
of his shadow at that moment when the shadow
of an ordinary man was as long
as the man was tall.

Tom Thomson snorts at philosophers.
He has never touched a tape measure.
He eyeballs every measurement,
and is astoundingly accurate.

He measures once, cuts once.
He speaks seven languages. He has perfect pitch.

4.
A hesitant breeze brings mist from the north.
The location of the sun during the past
three days is a matter of some controversy.
The lake is stiffening with trout. They are pouring
in from all over. The sound of a paddle
entering and pushing the water aside
slowly corrupts the silence.

Tom Thomson stops, lets go the paddle,
reaches over the side and makes
a secret mark on a rock.
The mark indicates that this is a place
Tom Thomson has been, and will come to again.

Have you ever seen a man murdered?
Once. I saw it in a mirror.
And did he remind you of your father?
I can't answer that question. Nor any other.

5.
Tom Thomson likes to pull a trout from the water
and fry it up with parsley and wild tomatoes.
The recipe is from his favorite restaurant
on Yonge Street in Toronto. Tom Thomson
eats there once a year. He does not need
a reservation. He has left a secret
mark upon the door.

What is Tom Thomson's secret mark?
What does it look like?

I can't tell you.

Come on.

Let me tell you something: the trout
that come to the place where water meets water
are the same trout every year.
They are not born. They do not die.

Impossible.

All I can do is tell you.

What of the sign. Can you give me a hint?

I already have.

Tell me something.
Is that Tom Thomson playing the piano?

That is not Tom Thomson playing the piano.
Tom Thomson plays no instrument. He does not
sing. He knows no poetry.
He can't even read. Tom Thomson
spends each night alone, listening to the phonograph,
looking at old family photos. Or so they say.

Balkan Journal, 1944

August 25. I've really had very little chance to pick up this notebook in the three weeks since I took up my new duties in this village with the unpronounceable name of Asvestohori. My group is officially assigned the task of distributing medical supplies to our troops quartered here and the task of supervising the municipal water service that is supposed to keep our water pure in this region. Except for part of one day a week, the work here is endless, with only the occasional hour or two of free time, usually after the night has blackened our barracks. Those of us who have been transferred from other Wehrmacht units are put to work at the most menial assignments outside our official duties, as though we are new recruits meant to earn our right to belong to the society of our veteran companions, some of whom have been in this war for a much shorter time than I have. Even among those who have been transferred here there is an order of priority, with the newest arrivals assigned the meanest work. Only soldiers of the rank of private—sometimes no more than children—work under me. And much of the work I supervise as corporal in my unit is the most humiliating kind, sometimes the garbage area in the kitchen, sometimes the toilet area, which is hardly more than a series of filthy tiled holes in the ground.

My official medical duties are a relief: two periods a day in the supply room arranging bottles and packages, and one or more trips a week into the countryside to help with purifying our water supply. These trips have the feel of a brief escape from prison. We are given the whole of a morning to complete our work, because the officer in charge of our group is himself in no hurry to return to our unit in Asvestohori. He likes to linger over a coffee and a cognac in the village of Hortiati in the foothills of the same mountain that rose behind us south of here during my days in our Salonika headquarters near the village of Arsakli. After we have added our chemicals to the water supply, the two of us from the lower ranks are assigned to the local first aid station for an hour or so of treating the Hortiati villagers for minor injuries. Then, while our leader sips his second cognac, we are allowed to wander in the village as we please for a while or walk the fields below in the neighborhood of the water source, our official excuse for being in the open countryside so pleasurably long. I mostly walk the fields. There is a high point above the ruined aqueduct that marks our source, and from this high point I can see across the valley to the meadow where I used to spend the only hours during my two years in this country when I could know the kind of peace I left behind in our valley outside Graz. That high point is where I take my rest, for as long as I can bear it.

My several trips into the countryside have also given me a chance to talk with the men of the municipal water service in a mix of my broken Greek and their broken German, men of some education, it seems, whom we are meant to escort and supervise in this operation. I've learned more than I choose to tell the others from these bits and pieces of conversation during those moments when we stop briefly to escape the sun under a tree or in the shade of our armored car. It is clear that some of these Greeks not only fear that Germany has lost the war but that we will be leaving their country soon and they will be in danger for having worked at our side, the enemy's side. I try to convince them that surely their work as water purifiers will be considered by the local people to have been necessary work, but either my primitive Greek is inadequate or their cynicism is too deep to allow simple words to penetrate their gloom.

I don't argue with them about the question of when we will be leaving. Every single day rumors pass through our unit that our army's departure has already been decreed, and no one doubts any longer that this is so. There are also rumors that Paris has fallen to the French, that the Bulgarians have withdrawn from the war so that our northeastern flank is now exposed, that there is total mobilization at home. This tells us how desperate the situation must be since there is surely no one left to mobilize other than children and old men. The only question now is when we will be leaving Greece: this month, the next, in any case certainly before Christmas.

Is it too much to hope that I may be in Graz by then, dear Lotte? Dare I hope that? I'm not sentimental about Christmas, not anymore, but I remember that you are. Forgive me if I recall how much you cried when you were eight and they denied you the role of the Virgin Mary in your school play because you were considered too small to hold the infant Christ in your arms. And so instead you became a pouting angel at the back of the set with one wing broken and a look in your eyes that would have turned any watching shepherd into stone. Then, when you finally got the role three years later, you still cried about it, though that was because you couldn't stop brooding over whether you were good enough for the part. The worry that this brought into your sweet face made you a perfect grieving Mary even if it was at your child's birth rather than his death.

Do you mind if I continue to amuse myself by pretending to write you in this secret way? Since I am certain that nobody will ever see this soiled little notebook, there surely can be no harm in my being playful about these things that mattered so much to you then, during the intimacy of our childhood together. Does your belief matter so much to you still? I wish I could talk to you about it as I once could, but I'm afraid I would be no use to you in that way any longer. If there is a God, He is not with us here. Our God has forsaken us or was never with us from the start. In either case, we are now alone in a wilderness of our own making.

September 4. I must write about what has happened. I think it's the only way I can hold myself together, keep my mind from going out of control. I have more time now than I could want, because things have fallen apart here, and for the moment I seem to have been forgotten. I sit by myself hour after hour waiting for some new assignment, but none has come. My old assignment, the best part of it, vanished last Saturday, our usual day for purifying the water below the village of Hortiati. There was an ambush, and Naegele was killed. Naegele is the sergeant who has been with our medical group far longer than any of us and who would always go with me into the village to treat those villagers who wait for us each week outside the first aid station. He had been doing that for months, more than a year, and the villagers had come to think of him as some kind of healing saint even if he was a German soldier. They would kneel before him sometimes, cross themselves, much to his embarrassment. He was only a little older than me, but the war had turned his blond hair mostly white. Everyone in that village must have known Naegele by now. I can't believe any one of them would have lain in wait to kill him, though I've come to believe anything is possible in this war. Some say it was the Communists who did it, a guerrilla unit camped on the mountain. The one certain thing about what happened is that Naegele is now dead, and because of that, the village of Hortiati is burned to the ground in retaliation.

I can't help but think that this was my fault. I was assigned to drive the car. When the ambush wounded our officer, Leutnant Ebert, who was riding in the back seat, Naegele opened the front door to see what was going on and was shot in the face. I pulled him back inside and drove off first in the direction we were headed, toward the aqueduct, then realized my mistake and swung around to head back the way we'd come. The shooting was going on, but it must have been aimed at the car on the far side of the road belonging to the municipal water service. Leutnant Ebert was moaning in the back seat, so I knew he was still alive, but I could tell that Naegele was dead beside me even though I couldn't bring myself to look at what was left of his face.

I drove on like a maniac until I came to the place where the road splits. I took the left branch heading toward Arsakli and our old headquarters, then decided that was too far to go with a wounded man and backed out to head toward Asvestohori. I stopped to look at Naegele, then took off my shirt to cover his head, and when I looked in back I saw that Leutnant Ebert had his eyes closed and was white, but he was still breathing, and there was no blood near his mouth. I decided to keep going. As we arrived at the outskirts of Asvestohori, Leutnant Ebert came to suddenly and asked where we were. I told him, then asked him if we should stop to work on his wound. He said it could wait, it was only his arm, grazed by a bullet. When we reached the guardhouse, he was out of the car and past the guard before I could get out to help him. He picked up the phone in the guardhouse, I suppose to sound the alarm. I called one of the guards over to help me carry Naegele into the shade.

I know now that I should have kept going on the road to Arsakli as I started to. It would have taken us much longer to get help, yes, but that might have been long enough to save the villagers in

Hortiati. That is what Naegele would have done. Instead I took the short route for the benefit of Leutnant Ebert. And that hardly gave the villagers, in any case too few of them, enough time to escape into the mountains before he sounded his alarm. He must have got through to Arsakli by phone from the guardhouse, got through to the intelligence headquarters which is responsible for counter-resistance operations, because the retaliation started almost immediately. The trucks in our compound had begun to fill up with men before we'd managed to wrap Naegele in a blanket and carry him inside the mess hall. And by the time we did, the famous Sergeant Schubert had arrived outside our compound with his specialists from the Partisan Pursuit Unit and their Greek informers. We all knew something terrible was going to happen. There were too many trucks and armored cars lined up for a simple counter-ambush operation. And it happened, within the hour. And while it happened, all I could do was sit on the floor beside Naegele's body and hold my head and try to understand why he was the one who'd been killed rather than Leutnant Ebert or me. Naegele would have shot Leutnant Ebert before he would have let him do harm to that village so late in this war we've lost.

They took me there yesterday. An investigation team, two officers and their aides, arrived from the intelligence unit in Arsakli to interview Leutnant Ebert. Since he wasn't thought healthy enough to ride in a car, I became the only witness who could show them where the ambush had taken place. One of the officers from Arsakli was the same thin-faced Nazi with the quiet voice who had questioned me last month at the intelligence headquarters in the schoolhouse, but he pretended not to recognize me and I saw no reason to recognize him. The other officer, even taller and large-nosed, was said to be the one who turned in his counter-partisan intelligence reports with a single *W* for his signature that was so slanted and shapeless he no doubt hoped it would serve to hide him from history.

I showed them where we'd been ambushed. That should have been enough, but they made me stay with them through their tour of the village beyond. There was little left that one would call a village—a few houses more or less untouched, most of them blackened shells, some ashes only. There was total silence in that place. The bodies of those who had been shot in the streets were mostly gone. We barely stopped to look at those still left, men and women of all ages. The smell of charcoal and burned flesh was everywhere, but especially on one street near the center of the village where the bakery used to be. We heard that Schubert came back from the reprisal bragging to our men about how he had saved ammunition by filling that bakery with all the stragglers he could round up, dozens and dozens, then sealing the door and burning them to death. Nobody went very far into that street and nobody took notes.

The investigation team turned back before we'd reached the upper edge of the village. They said there was nothing more to be seen that hadn't been seen already, but the real reason was that one of the aides had become sick from the smell, and there was talk of possible infection in the air. Also, we were being watched from the hills. One of the officers, the one who pretended not to know me, said he was certain he'd heard the sound of a shepherd's flute on the mountainside above the village, and this made him realize suddenly that we were completely exposed. He'd taken it for a signal. I'd heard it, too, and I'd thought it a sound that could chill the gods.

Rave

He says, You have to know, huh?
Well, I listen to it because
I can't stumble into bliss,
Can't kill myself with sugar.

It makes my head hurt, she says.
I feel plugged into a box of wires
Dangling loose. Sampled rigmarole
In a gallery of Donatien Alphonse

François. He sits in the booth
Beside her, shaking his head.
You don't hear right, he says.
The re-echo has you on tenterhooks.

I love you. But that vociferous
Thump-thump sounds like a flywheel
Rattling around in an unbolted nogginbox,
& I'm ready to kill somebody, she says.

NICOLE KRAUSS

Your Watch

82

It slipped my wrist, vanished in the street dark with steps
of no one I know, and late, and late. Picked up, dropped
in a stranger's pocket where the hours, yours, mean nothing but kept
time. I never asked whether you wore it then, crossing the street
when a car flung out of the rain. From now on—or from that last,
casual minute without a glance when I was released
into the future and you, at that same instant, turned back—
I will be late.

Common Blue

Their eggs are laid on lupine. Tiny jade
hairstreaks I could easily mistake for dew.
Too precious. Too incidental,
and besides that, blue, these trills that flounce
in my potato patch, drawn
from dryland origins to the domestic
stain of water from my hose.
What an old woman would study, I think
as you hand me the guidebook, distracted
by the replica of a parasol
growing out of a bleached cow pie.
The Siamese kitten with his butterfly eyes
comes running, his mouth full
of swallowtail, his breath smelling of borax
and sugar I have poured
over the ant hills in the garden.
He is young and intent on eating poison.
We bushwhack through Paradise,
what is there to say except to lament
the daily evidence of its passing.
How the common blues scatter from my shade.
And you, so fragile, so sick, so thin,
your diet restricted, keep pointing out
the bearded face of larkspur.
When the angels fell, a fifteenth-century bishop says,
there were 133, 306, 668 of them.
It takes us all afternoon to cross the field.
The body, it is so sad what happens to it.
If you fell, you would dry up instantly.
But these are not angel wings
who disguise themselves as leaf or shred of bark,
who are named after the stops
in meaning our language must make room for:

the comma whose wings look battered,
or the violet underside of the question mark.
To keep the mind from clenching, you say,
is the main thing. Even the most
beautiful days always seem to have death in them.
As Valentinus said; our fall into love and sleep.
You especially like the dark alpines
with their furred bodies and lack of marking.
And the sulphurs, yellowed scraps that fall
from a myth of origin that doesn't include us.
When we find them, we will wonder
who is still alive. We speak of our souls with such
surface ease. But who will take such care for us?
You bend and bend to the scrappy blue sea,
your back turned to the moon fluttering above you.
I have been thinking so much of strength
this week, yours and mine, I mean,
the field of attention that can be strengthened.

Cleanness

It was his father's wedding day. Roland had flown into London the night before and slept at the hotel off Russell Square where he'd stayed during the last days of his mother's illness. The ceremony, at the parish church near his father's new house in Suffolk, was set for noon; reception at the house to follow. Roland woke late and found to his surprise that he had had an erotic dream. He tried to remember it, but the attempt itself scattered the last traces still lingering in his head.

He cleaned off its physical residue in the shower, then dressed carefully in front of the mirror: his father had always been a stickler for tradition, and the words *formal attire* had been printed on the invitation.

The rented outfit, which came complete with gray top hat, silk tie, starched shirt, and even a red carnation, fitted him well, and in spite of the absurd tails hanging halfway down his legs, Roland was pleased with what he saw in the mirror.

He set off across London in a green Citroën—also rented—and was soon on the motorway. It was a bright day; cool, with a few hooked scratch marks of cloud crisscrossing the blue. *Cirrus Uncinus,* he said to himself. His father, a naturalist, had made him learn the names of clouds when he was a boy, and he still remembered them.

The old man was in his seventies now. His bride, Rosemary, wasn't much over thirty. In another man Roland might have been surprised at the gulf, but not in his father. Wiry and agile, with thick silver hair swept back from his forehead, sharp eyes still fiercely scrutinizing the world from his buzzard-like face, he had conceded little more than a kind of flinty hardening to the passage of time.

Roland had been introduced to Rosemary at a drinks party on his last visit. She was a biologist, and had met his father on a scientific expedition to Tierra del Fuego. She was an intelligent-looking woman with an interesting face that made Roland think of a

particular kind of craftsman's tool—a planishing hammer, was it?—
in its smoothly molded planes and concavities; its look of having
been evolved to perform some highly specific, complex function.

She had come towards him with an expression that had in it
both shyness and something propitiatory. She seemed to want to
convey to him her innocence of anything that might smack of an
intent to interfere in his relations with his father, to assure him of
her friendliness, and even in some way to ask his forgiveness for
anything in the situation that he might find uncomfortable. They
hadn't talked for long, but he had left feeling well-disposed
towards her.

He had seen her one more time on that visit. She'd come to
London for the day, and had rung him at his hotel to invite him
for lunch. They ate at a Greek restaurant and afterwards spent an
hour wandering through the quiet streets around Hanover
Square. Again the sensitivity, the propitiatory manner that
soothed Roland and put him at his ease. He felt relaxed, and in
response to her tactful but evidently sincere curiosity, talked to
her quite volubly about his life—the well-paid banking job in
Brussels that his father disapproved of (he disapproved of any
profession that wasn't explicitly dedicated to the betterment of
the human race), his unraveling marriage, his childhood.

His mother's unhappy existence had ended in a hospital not far
from where they were walking, and as they approached the shab-
bier streets that had become so familiar to him from his daily vis-
its, he began to feel all the harsh emotions of that period resurrect
themselves inside him. Whether by chance or by some peculiar
power of intuition, it was just then that Rosemary began to ques-
tion him about his mother. Caught off his guard, which had been
firmly up since her death, Roland had found himself delivering a
long, fervent speech full of all the sorrow and exasperation that
had lain pent up inside him for the past three years. Without crit-
icizing his father, he tried to convey his irrational but nevertheless
profound belief in a secret symbiosis between his father's vigor
and his mother's steady decline. However much the old man
harangued her for not pursuing a career, for not seeing a psychia-
trist when she became depressed, for drinking too much, for
smoking after she was diagnosed with cancer, there was some part
of him (and for this Roland admitted he had no evidence beyond

his own highly subjective instincts) that required absolutely that she remain on the downward slide, just as a healthy plant requires the steady disintegration of the organisms in the soil around it in order to thrive. And by whatever convoluted action of the psyche, his irreproachable concern for her welfare had precisely the opposite effect of what was apparently intended. It kept her in thrall to her own failure.

Within about twenty minutes of leaving the motorway, Roland realized that he was lost. His father's map, which plunged from A to Z without regard for any of the opportunities for deviation that country roads offer in between, no longer corresponded to anything Roland could see.

He drove on, hoping to recognize a name on a signpost: without luck. Passing some houses, he considered stopping and asking for directions, but he felt awkward at the idea of going up a stranger's garden path in his wedding regalia, and before he could make up his mind to do it, the houses were behind him.

He realized that unless he found himself soon he would be late for the wedding, which would not go down well with the old man. By now, though, he was deep in the country. Fields of ripe barley lay on either side of him. There were a few barns here and there, but no houses. Small, unmarked roads appeared, each one necessitating a brief debate as to whether or not to explore it, so adding further to his consternation. Finally he came to the entrance of a driveway with the name of a farm on a sign.

The driveway twisted sharply down through a wood, then came out into a bare brown field with rows of scaly cabbage stumps. The unmistakable, offal-like smell of pigs blew in through the car window, though another quarter of a mile passed before he came to the gate of the farm itself. He parked to the side of the gate. The elegant Gallic contours of the Citroën looked almost as out of place here as he himself did in his tails and red carnation. Through the gate was a rundown courtyard of pigsties with a hundred or more pigs—gray and hairy with pink patches—rooting and snuffling inside them. As Roland walked past, they crowded forward to the iron bars, making loud, harsh squeals and grunts. Their sties were several inches deep in slop. Huge mounds of refuse were piled in the corners.

Not just the pigs themselves, but everything in the courtyard was covered in mud: buckets, bits of machinery, a small caravan occupied by chickens, even the chickens themselves. There was a forlorn oak tree with mud-covered leaves, and a wheelbarrow so caked with mud it looked as though it had been made out of papier-mâché.

He picked his way with care to the entrance of the farmhouse, and knocked. A woman wearing a short-sleeved dress and house slippers came to the door. She looked him up and down. He explained that he was on his way to a wedding and had got lost.

"Oh dear. I better get you a map. Come in."

She brought him into the kitchen, where she found a map and spread it on the table. She was about forty; large, with plump, pale arms. Her body in its thin cotton covering gave off a powdery odor—part perfume, part cigarette ash. Her eyes had a becalmed expression, almost dazed, but every now and then settling on Roland with a soft attentiveness.

"Who is it getting married, then?"

"My father."

"Ah. That's nice."

They found a route on the map. Thanking her for her help, Roland turned to leave. As he did, he saw a man standing in the doorway, holding a live white rabbit by the ears. Both the man and the rabbit were staring at him with expressions of amazement.

"He's lost his way," the woman explained. "He's going to his father's wedding."

The man said nothing. Roland edged out of the door past him, giving him a nod, which the man ignored. As Roland left he heard a crunch and thud, and a moment later a white rabbit head, still wearing its look of amazement, sailed past him into one of the pigsties. The pigs converged on it in a cacophony of squeals. Roland noticed that a drop of blood from the severed head had splashed onto his polished black shoe. He turned back to the house, perturbed by the farmer's aggressiveness, but the man had gone inside.

The gate out to the drive where the Citroën was parked was now blocked by a gigantic red tractor. Roland stopped, jarred by the sight into what seemed to be a deep rift of memory. Where had he seen such a tractor before? He had the sense of having recently seen a tractor exactly like this one, though since this was the first time he had been outside a city in years, it was hard to imagine where it might have been. Even so, there was something familiar about it.

As he moved on towards it, he realized he wouldn't be able to squeeze past it without dirtying his suit. He looked for another way out. On either side of him was thick, wet-looking black mud. A little way forward on his left, however, some planks had been laid down in a line leading to a gap in a brick wall. He stepped onto the planks, and walked gingerly along to investigate.

As he did, he thought again of the farmer's behavior. It occurred to him that the man might have been a jealous husband wondering whether he had surprised his wife in the middle of a clandestine meeting with her lover. Dressed as he was, he perhaps had presented a certain archetypal, if also ludicrous, image that a jealous temperament might have found irresistibly suspicious. Then, too, Roland surmised as he picked his way along the planks, perhaps he did have the face of an adulterer. A man's more significant deeds might perhaps have a way of imprinting themselves on his anatomy, if in a manner visible only to the unconscious eye of other people. Had his marital infidelities left their signature on his flesh? Had the farmer dimly perceived it? Was he at some level even correct in his appraisal of the situation; that Roland did have designs on his wife? In a detached, clinical manner, Roland brought the woman back into his mind, imagined being in bed with her, was reassuringly unaroused, smiled to himself at the absurdity of it all, then suddenly remembered where he had seen the tractor before. It was what he had opened his eyes to on the nursery floor where he and the children's Dutch nanny had first had sex. Unlike the one here at the farm, it was a toy, pedal-powered, but for an instant it had seemed vast and strangely menacing, perhaps because his three-year-old son was riding it.

By this point Roland had come to the gap in the wall at the end of the planks and seen that the wall itself enclosed a pool full of viscous greenish liquid that smelled like the contents of an open septic tank. There was no means of getting to the grass beyond it, and he turned to walk back. It was at this moment that the memory of the tractor had suddenly come to him, bringing with it a great wave of anxiety that seemed to contain in it the whole calamity of his marriage—the apparently inconsolable hurt he had inflicted on his wife, the silentness that had fallen on their young child, the bitter dismantling of the home—all of it surging through him with a force that for a moment overwhelmed him. He missed his footing on the plank. Groping at air to regain his balance, he fell backwards into the stinking pool.

A moment of absolute surrender followed. It was oddly luxurious, and he was aware of extending it for as long as he could. Although the day was cool, the liquid was warm, and in this state of surrender, what he felt seeping through his jacket and trousers wasn't wholly unpleasant. He looked at the old farm buildings around him, the crops beyond, the sky overhead: for a while he felt almost blissful. It was only as he hoisted himself out of the pool, rising from it like a swamp animal dripping slime, that he began to feel the true foulness of his condition. There was no pain, not even any great physical discomfort. But the sensation of a vile uncleanness both soaking into him and emanating out from him was inexpressibly horrible. He trudged back through the mud (what need now for the planked walkway?) towards the gate blocked by the squatting tractor. There before him, he saw what he had managed to conceal from himself before: just to the side of the main gate was another little one, which he could have passed through without any risk to his attire.

Tearing up clumps of dock (*Rumex Crispus*), he did what he could to wipe himself clean. He lined the seat of the Citroën with a protective layer of stalks and leaves before sitting down on it. In this manner, reeking, oozing greenish muck, he resumed his journey.

He was more than an hour late by the time he reached his father's village. Coming to the church, he saw that the wedding service was already over, and he drove on to the house.

This was a large building of brick and cobblestones. A rounded glass conservatory, filled no doubt with his father's specimens, protruded gracefully from the ample front. A brass band was playing in a marquee with fluttering pennants at the back of the wide lawn, where a couple of hundred guests were being served champagne. Under the shaggy arms of a cedar, long trestle tables had been set up, garlanded with flowers.

Large family gatherings had always unnerved Roland. From an early age he had associated them with all the more troubling aspects of his mother's personality: the outrageous remarks—cruel, snobbish, or simply bizarre—that any group above a certain critical mass seemed guaranteed to elicit from her; and then later the drunken outbursts of weeping, cursing, even violence, that his father's response of dignified silence served only to fan to ever more destructive heights.

He thought of the strange way his mother's image had been transfigured in his own consciousness. Alive, she had been a perpetual source of pain and humiliation—hatred even. Dying, she had aroused a kind of morbid solicitousness in him, strong enough that he had taken two months off from his job to look after her as she moved from her flat to the hospital and then to the crematorium. Dead, she had undergone a final change in his imagination, turning into something frail, blossomlike, but enduring, for which he bore unexpected tenderness and love. He heard her voice, sad and low, as if she were present again beside him. *It isn't me,* she would say after each new attempt to make something of her life had been abandoned. The volunteer work, the college administration job, the gift shop . . . *It just isn't me . . .* A familiar dim helplessness washed through him. At moments he could glimpse something almost intentional behind his own calamities; an obscure, insidious solidarity . . . Abruptly, the dream he had woken from that morning in his hotel came back to him: the woman in it had been his mother. A sharp pang of dismay went through him. *A wet dream about my own mother,* he thought, almost wearily. *What next?*

Clammy, still smelling badly, with bits of straw and torn leaves sticking to the slime on his suit, he made his way towards the guests. Before he reached them, he caught sight of his father: as ever a little shorter than he remembered him, but his silver hair gleaming with that curious vitality that had the effect of making you briefly question whether you mightn't have got things the wrong way round; whether silver wasn't after all the color of youth, while brown, black, and blond were the colors hair turned in old age. Beside him stood Rosemary, slim and erect in her white outfit, her veil pinned back, flowers and seed-pearls gleaming in the silk and lace of her dress.

Moving towards the crowd of guests, Roland had the impression of entering the locus of a single, vast, living organism. The old man had always had a gift for ceremony, display; for all those occasions requiring a particular complex of forces to be summoned into harmonious form. University chancellors regularly consulted him on their processionals and jubilees, as did the organizers of village fetes. What radiant entity had he brought forth here? As Roland approached, its epidermis seemed to shrink from him, as though fine hairs or antennae had detected something inimical to its own rustling brilliance.

His father saw him.

"Ah. There you are," he said, not unkindly. His manner, too, was less forbidding in reality than it was in Roland's imagination. But when he saw the state Roland was in, he stiffened.

"What in heaven's name—"

"I'm sorry—"

As Roland moved towards him, he stepped back, drawing Rosemary with him. She pulled her arm free, however, and looked at Roland with the same warmth in her eyes as he had seen when he first met her. For a moment it seemed she hadn't noticed his condition, but when he heard his father say, "Rosemary, be careful, he's filthy," and saw her continue on towards him, it occurred to him that she didn't care. Over his own swamp-smell he caught the fragrance of lilies-of-the-valley. She put her long, silk-furled arms about him and drew him close, her white dress surely staining in great oval blotches from his oozing suit. In her embrace he thought again of his dream; his mother's incontinent body whole, supple in his hands; her naked breasts warm and sweet in his mouth. Appalling! And yet as he stood there he felt as if he were on the point of being cleansed of the confusions, the glutinous horrors of his day, and instead of letting Rosemary go, he drew her tighter to him, burying his head in her sweet-smelling shoulder, while dimly beyond her he could hear his father tutting and fussing. And a strange elation rose through him, as though the great miasma that had hung upon his life so long it had come to seem a part of his own nature, might after all be about to lift.

Middle-Class Regalia as Iconographic Vanitas

Desire zeroing in on that Furby eBay auction
      while smut chat gets caught up
in the Hegelian carpet role—the secrets of your life
      scrawled on Post-it notes that fell
off of your dash—a pack of Lucky Strikes stairmastered into
      Liberty's verdigrised torch—
Ellis Island heavier than an oil freighter grounded
      in Coos Bay, grenade bundles
dropped into the cargo hold where stowaways and rough trade
      are peddled inside a dream
disfigured by grief, our heels on poesy's throat, our wants
      enclosed in the Dantesque windows
of Saks Fifth Avenue where pigeons peck at dried-out crusts
      like fifty-something biddies
trying to take their power back, their bulging pocketbooks
      a Bakhtinian carnival
scatterpiece hauled away by troika or by gitney ride
      through Central Park—tenderness
staged beside Ming vases of doubtful provenance that puts
      everything on its mettle
from the prints of Lorrain to the odes of Keats—not buying
      the house but buying the view—
the *zazen* of stained glass undoing ambition's talons
      claw by claw—stocks and futures
traded in for a Byzantine reliquary housing splinters
      and a nail from a True Cross.

I Live Where the Leaves Are Pointed

at my head and my heart, knife-tips green
in a gasoline-doused garden. From the tire
store behind the house, leering mechanics
glaze my window with saliva. I sit at the end
of the couch and point my finger angrily,
wag it in the face of forever. I sit back on
my haunches and sniff the air. Please note:
the earth is no less sulfur than usual. It's not
nothing I'm waiting for, not as if there's no
reason I've done my hair at last. If I weren't
waiting, why would I be so impatient?
I don't drink whiskey to relax.
And there is someone I wouldn't mind seeing
dead. But when I comb my hair and stay
up all night, it's not as if I'm trying to meet
someone. The days can travel without me.
The landlord can mow the lawn in shifts,
his pink face an obscene balloon caught
by the noose of his collar—I'll sleep through
the motor. And you can bet my dreams bloom
stranger than hallucination. I take my life
like this. Poems grow from my skull while
vines creep the tire store wall: slowly, certainly.
When they made soap, they had me in mind.

800 Acres on the Plains

High Lonesome tipped back his hat
and his horses snorted. Maybelle nodded,
her teacher's smile a wild azalea
in miles of cactus. My uncle's buckboard

groaned to a stop, in town for flour
and grease and beans. All that, decades ago,
before he taught me how to cowboy. Five summers
we broke broncs, patched fences cut by hunters,

shot coyotes hobbling and starved.
He never married after Maybelle died,
no one to carry on the herd but me, a summer nephew.
Uncle Carl taught me to rope and brand,

leap back when the calf jumped up.
Carl taught me to shoot, a mile-long whine
across a mile of pasture. His ribs were gaunt
as an old bull's, alone on an August range.

While I flew back from Vietnam, he died.
His saddles and gates were still the same.
My wife and I moved out to the ranch,
wild windmills whirring, the same bad drought.

Our children left home years ago,
leaving us rocking at night under stars,
far from them all, from the wall in Washington
where Don and Kelly and Harper's names

are carved in granite black as the plains
out there—no moon, tonight, no one but us
to hear the coyotes, the squeal of a field mouse
caught by an owl, flapping back to the barn.

A Testicular Self-Examination

*The Rio Grande should be repaired sooner or later because it's
a shame what happened to it which is not pretty. Irrigation
and all and no sturgeon any more and pubic hairs
and pollution.*
—Harve Benedict, English 12, Elfego Baca High School

O hundreds and hundreds of Harves, your writing should have been the death of me. It should have been.

In my memory I picture you and our off-white high-school cinderblock classroom, the stinking heated air, imbalanced orange plastic chairs and desks, manic-twitching-riccocheting fluorescence, spittled spatter-pattern tiles, and smeared chalkboards. More alone with my lesson plans than I had planned, I pay tribute, seat you, take attendance, mark you present but gone.

Gone. And missed.

Even the ass-kissing or dispassionate or self-obsessed wasted-slacker slumming hopeless worst of you Harves are still dangerously present in me.

For the record, I should mark down that my grade books were amiss because I made a place across twelve columns to record my sales, your costs, and, at my whim, the other matters at hand.

I had slots in my books for the good shit, for the shit, for the rewrite second shot, for the wasted second shot. I had a slot I could make you fit.

I have all the grade books. In thirty years of teaching they are the only books I wrote.

You knew firsthand my forms of insult to The Teaching Profession, so you would understand that I remember you best just when I have my pants around my ankles, my testicles in hand, fumbling with my most ordinary means of communication, my praxis and true praxis, my imagined spheres of influence, my twin inadequate vocabularies, my theses, my parallel narratives and my pure lyric impulses, my flesh's synonyms and soul's antonyms. My syllabi.

My syllabi. There, that clarifies, that has a ring.

I willed the essays you wrote to define but not defy the audience. I wanted your words, I willed them to have the true ring; you wished them to ring true. And because I had been taught the dry, exhausted world would operate neither on beauty's truth nor truth's beauty, I knew from the beginning what curriculum I would teach you.

So, I repeat, I repeat myself as I self-examine, passing my fingertips like blind mandibles over the puckered, seamed curtain of my scrotum to discover the drama growing upon the drama within. Oh, I imagine I see you, see your eyes spin, the light in them dimming, as they always did when, in my less naked days, I exercised my prerogatives and lectured at you, poking parts of the enlarged diagrammed sentence I pinned to the cork strip at the top of the scored chalkboard.

Are you as embarrassed as I am by this admission into evidence of my two mortgages, two secret business files, yang and yang, And and Ampersand, my letter home and letter back, my Brothers Grimm, my Brothers Grimm? Embarrassing.

It is embarrassing. Goddamn.

It is—and it was then. O hundreds and hundreds of Harves, I bent your attention from the words you had written to what I called "the matter at hand" to which we gave our concentration whether or not your essay was a yelp in the dark, a wild song meant to break you from the ranks of the marching.

I dynamited the secret daily deepening love for learning inside any of you who had the elemental need for beauty and brutality within. Strictly according to my orders, you obediently rode your hands and the nubs of your pens over the surface of the page in order to not enter, not swim in where your unsleeping secrets and first and final doubts might appear unhidden.

Your sparking faces reignite in my memory, and will not be drowned out as I drowned them out then. Self-loathing, self-loving, self-avoiding, I am self-examining, self-examining my classifieds, my want ads, questioning, and indulging, indulging and indulging my excesses of self-intimacy.

My motives will never be unugly, will they? No one knows as you do that what compassion I lacked made me ask you back any question you asked.

In a race against you dambreakers, I made dams. Wanting language to have use, I demanded you learn how to change its natural course, to divert it, drain every untamed cubic foot.

Of course. You knew, know that.

Do you remember? When you picture me, is this what you picture?

Showered and powdered. A midday desert storm makes the bathroom light fixture tremble, and the water swirling down the drain flashes at me like a whip snake.

The lights in my home are lowered and curtains drawn. I know my curriculum, my medical routine as one of "the predisposed," as one of cancer's pupils.

Goddamned. Oh, I do not want to remember, but I remember the hundreds of sentence-suffering student conferences with my chipped, unbalanced metal desk between us in my designated space of the giant communal school office.

There was weed and fast-food smell on you, Harve. Eyes and cheeks blood-webbed, the backs of your neck and hands sunburned and your palms blistered.

Nothing on either side of "because" seemed to flow right for you. O Harve, Harve Discussion-Killer, Harve Chain-Yanker—son of fourth-generation Mesilla Valley cotton farmers—class of '90? '91?—second-sem junior Goth metalhead brilliant nonachiever— emerald goatee, emerald short spiked hair, mucous-coated skull ring hanging from your septum.

You wrote, The Rio Grande should be fixed because it's a fuckin shame what happened to it.

"Harve," I said, "what part should be repaired? It's a big river."

You said, "The whole thing." I said, "It's a long river."

You said, "Repair it, then. Don't fix it."

"It's best to focus, Harve." "Fuck you," you said.

"And when—you should say when." I asked, "Well, Harve?"

"Yeah? Yeah, yeah."

"Listen. Can you put 'when' in?"

You said, "Fuck you." I said, "Would you put 'when' in?"

You pinched the feet of the crucified Christ on your homemade earring, and you kind of put "when" in: The Rio Grande should be repaired sooner or later because it's a fuckin shame what happened to it which is not pretty.

That's better, I said, not believing my own words. Believing only in the complete sentence, I disliked your added fragment, which you would not change: Irrigation and all and no sturgeon any more and pubic hair and pollution.

O Harve, O hundreds and hundreds—with any luck, you haven't thought of me for years. I wish this for you: that I am dismissed, expelled, that I never come to mind, that I am your lost but replaceable crutch tips, your unrefillable prescriptions, the lecture notes you would not take, the higher grade you would not get.

O you hundreds and hundreds of Harves missing the "because" gene, I have poured you in and poured you out of my bifocal lenses, I have insisted that we bow to the matter at hand, the curriculum, the curriculum, but I have needed, wanted your flooding truth to kill what I have been. For thirty years.

Now, I have my immutable troubles and truths, such as they are, unwarranted radials, good-as-new-unrebuilt-used hard disk drives, my riches, my riches, out in the poor light, though I understand that looking will not help me. I go by touch.

For thirty years I have made the same mean wrong wishes—to identify instead of know—to reach instead of search—and a third I could not or would not name: to put an end to anything that simply is. You, my matter at hand, my own overproductive, overeager metastasizing cells, have tumesced in me for three decades of daily sweet assault upon my most sacrosanct first principles of utility.

You have taught me. You have taught me.

How blessedly terrifying to search for and know you, the truths gathering, gathering within me. You have grown upon and will destroy me.

The Fix and the Fall

The fuzz knows the whiz
and vice versa. This leads to
cooperation.

Your average dick
is on the shake. A little
jack will make him right.

Count on a C-note
per man per day; if there's no
bad beefs, you're okay.

Once you've fixed the bull,
even when a mark blows, he'll
give you a pass-up.

Fit the fur the best
you can, but an airtight fix
is impossible.

We've all had bad falls:
the rapper won't stop yelling,
and the sham won't take.

He makes the sneeze. What's
next depends on how much scratch
you have in your seams.

Even if you're caught
dead to rights, with fall dough up
you'll stay out of stir.

No mob wants its hook
in the bucket, so they'll grind
up nickels and dimes.

Everyone's happy.
The button is squared, for now,
and the wire is sprung.

The Defenseless

We are not scaled.
We do not boast
horns,
or quills,
or wooly coats.
Our skin is pliable
and thin.
No fangs or scales
conceal our throats.

Worms regrow
their missing tails,
though tail is all they know
of limb.
A cat can close
her inner eye.
Ants hide beneath
their skeletons.
But humans,
scant of shell
or hide,
lead, unfazed,
with the underside.

The Scuffle of the Small

The overrated owe
a great debt to the little:
the pinpoint feet of shrimp
unleash the tide pool billows.

The mismatched flecks within the rock
make granite glitter.
Could the gnat impart
the summer with her shimmer?

Each spring the tightness of the soil
is tirelessly relieved
by the boring of a worm:
she dares the roots to breathe.

Likewise the fleeting glance
reshuffles our attention.
The awkward and unrhymed
wheedle in and loosen

with such resolve that all our gaps
and solitudes are filled.
It is the scuffle of the small
that stirs the silt.

I Am Not Seaworthy

I am not seaworthy.
Look how the fish mistake my hair
    for home.
I had a life, like you. I shouldn't be
    riding the sea.
I am not seaworthy.
Let me be earthbound; star fixed
mixed with sun and smacking air.
Give me the smile, the magic kiss
to trick little boy death of my hand.
I am not seaworthy. Look how the fish
    mistake my hair for home.

The Lacemaker

I am as you see
what most becomes me:
miles skipped
canceled trips
masters yet unmet.
Lace alone is loyal, sacred, royal, in control
of crimes stopped
by patterns of blood bred to best behavior.
As you see I am
what has become of me.

The Perfect Ease of Grain

The perfect ease of grain
time enough to spill
the flavor of a woman carried through the rain.

Honey-talk tongues
down home dreams
a rushed but shapely prayer.
Evening lips part to hush
questions raised at dawn.

The melon yields another slice.
Fingers understand.
Ecstasy becomes us all.
Red cherries become jam.

Deep juvenile sleep
a whistle trace
white shorelines in green air.
Welcome doors held open
when goodbye is "So long."

The perfect poise of grain
time enough to kill
the flavor of a woman remembered on a train.

The Town Is Lit

It's been suggested: well kept
lawns and fences, white porch swings and
toast by the fire.
It's been requested: puppies, a
window of blossoming pear trees and a
place for robins to nest.

But I know that somewhere, out there
the town is lit.
The players begin
to make music in all the cafés.
Clowns on wheels
linger to steal
foxes that click on the curb.
Lovers expecting
the night to protect them
the moon too far to disturb.
Trees in the park
dance after dark
to music in all the cafés.

It's been suggested: well kept
lawns and fences, white porch swings and
toast by the fire.
It's been requested: puppies, a
window of blossoming pear trees and a
place for the robins to nest.

But I know that somewhere, out there
Geminis split
Sagittarians kick
to the music in all the cafés.
Aquarians throw
gold on the floor
to rival the glitter it makes.

Pisces swim
over the rim
knowing they've got what it takes to
cut through the dark
get to the heart
of the music in all the cafés.

Coming To (in) America

It was one of those things
you just have to
believe to *see.*
Let's call him, Kenneth—
yes, Kenneth
Oboto—
sitting *statue still,*
no, say: *still as machete death*—
in a silk, leopard-skin
tutu blouse and skullcap,
Parade Magazine in hand—
on a green-slatted
Iowa City
park bench,
day-one,
freshman orientation—
like a beautiful, black-eyed
Rwandan pea
on a rolling wave
of new-flaxen corn—
no,
like a black, plaster
lawn-jockey—
(caught in the headlights), eyes
wide open onto
James Brady's: Interview
with Dan Rather,
(ruddy, red-blooded, American
as apple pie & shotguns
at a 4th of July
lynching—no,
picnic,
beside the Pedernales—)

exhorting:
What's the frequency,
Kenneth? What's
the frequency,
Kenneth!

The Playwright and the Blond Actress

A Play in One Act

commissioned by McCarter Theatre,
Princeton, New Jersey

PLAYWRIGHT, middle-aged
BLOND ACTRESS, childlike but about thirty

Lights up. The Playwright is typing on an old portable typewriter on a stool or a small raised table. His actions need not seem realistic. He faces the audience, brooding.

The Blond Actress appears at the rear, glimpsed through a scrim. She may also be veiled or wear something diaphanous over her face. Her clothing is white, and she is barefoot.

Blond Actress talks and laughs to herself. We need not hear her words clearly.

ACTRESS: ... promised. "Always love you." "Never write about you." He said! Oh, I knew ... But I didn't ... did I? (*Laughs.*)

PLAYWRIGHT: (*Has been typing rapidly with two fingers but now ceases.*) She's always in the way ... Oh God.

Blond Actress emerges with a flourish through the scrim, gliding rapidly behind the Playwright to the other side of the stage. A light, shrill ripple of laughter.

Playwright shivers. Has he heard? He removes the sheet of paper from the typewriter, hesitates, and crumples it. (As the Blond Actress mimes closing a window.) Playwright becomes warm, uncomfortable.

Playwright suddenly becomes excited, angry. He inserts another sheet of paper and quickly types a line or two.

PLAYWRIGHT: (*Voice raised.*) You did lie! Oh yes. When there wasn't yet any need.

Blond Actress moves behind the Playwright. Fluffs the back of his hair and eases away, giggling, as he turns and fails to see her.

ACTRESS: *That* again?

PLAYWRIGHT: (*An old argument.*) There was *never any need.* You debased us both, making me out to be...jealous. (*Pause.*) Who shut that window? (*Pause; in a louder voice.*) What about him?

Actress shakes her head vigorously, like a child.

PLAYWRIGHT: You know who I mean.

ACTRESS: (*Reluctantly, but in an earnest, breathless manner.*) It was that...magic in him...he could reach right *in*...

PLAYWRIGHT: (*Meanly.*) Busy fingers, eh?

ACTRESS: His eyes...

PLAYWRIGHT: Myopic, like mine. (*A beat.*) But he exploited you. As a woman.

ACTRESS: A woman? What do I care about myself as a *woman*...? I came to New York to *act.*

PLAYWRIGHT: Bullshit. You always gave him too much credit. The moth to the flame. I hate it, in interviews, you inflate his worth.

ACTRESS: Oh, but how could I...? He was like...you.

PLAYWRIGHT: (*Ignoring this; typing a few angry lines.*) Yes. What women do. Deflect attention from themselves, to inflate some self-important bastard.

ACTRESS: (*Struck by the insight.*) Oh. Is that what…?

PLAYWRIGHT: Darling, you knew how to act when you came here. You could have taught us all.

Actress shakes her head uncertainly.

PLAYWRIGHT: I hate that, too, the way you deliberately…misinterpret yourself.

ACTRESS: I do? Gee…

PLAYWRIGHT: Sabotage yourself.

ACTRESS: "Sabotage"…?

PLAYWRIGHT: You were a goddamned good actress when you came to New York. *He* didn't create you.

ACTRESS: (*Sudden laughter.*) *You* created me.

PLAYWRIGHT: Nobody created you. You were always yourself.

ACTRESS: But…who's that? (*Pause; twines hair around fingers.*) Well, I guess I knew…some things. When I made movies. I was reading Stanislaski…slavki. And the diary of…Nijinski.

PLAYWRIGHT: (*Gently corrects pronunciation.*) Nijinski.

ACTRESS: (*Suddenly upset.*) Don't you laugh at me!

PLAYWRIGHT: I'm not laughing at you.

ACTRESS: I see words on the page, I don't know how to say them. But I know what they *are.*

PLAYWRIGHT: Right. You always did.

ACTRESS: It's hard, though ... to know what you know. Until it happens. Like ... when I had to improvise? Like striking a match.

PLAYWRIGHT: You don't have to *know*. You were a natural.

ACTRESS: But I want to *know*!

PLAYWRIGHT: The hell with that, you were a natural actress from the start.

ACTRESS: Oh, hey! Why're you mad, Daddy?

PLAYWRIGHT: I'm only saying, darling, you were born with the gift. A kind of ... genius. You don't need theory. Forget Stanislavski. Nijinski. (*With disdain.*) *Him.*

ACTRESS: (*Quickly.*) I never think of him.

PLAYWRIGHT: (*Disgusted.*) Him messing with you ... your talent, your soul ... Somebody's big thumbs smearing ... breaking ... a butterfly's wings.

ACTRESS: Hey, I'm no butterfly. Feel my muscle? My leg here. I'm a dancer.

The Playwright turns as if to touch the Actress, who has moved away.

The Actress, restless, executes several dance steps.

PLAYWRIGHT: Bullshit theory is for somebody like him ... can't act, can't write.

ACTRESS: Kiss-kiss, Daddy? C'mon.

The Playwright rises to approach the Actress, who eludes him.

ACTRESS: Hey, listen: he wasn't my lover, really.

PLAYWRIGHT: What's that mean—"really"?

ACTRESS: Oh, he might've done some things, but it wasn't . . . Don't look at me like that, Daddy. That scares me. (*She seems genuinely scared.*)

PLAYWRIGHT: (*Calmly.*) What did he do?

ACTRESS: (*A giggle.*) Nothing actual.

PLAYWRIGHT: He . . . touched you?

ACTRESS: I guess. How d'you mean?

PLAYWRIGHT: As a man touches a woman.

ACTRESS: (*Drawing near, a quick caress.*) Mmmm. Like this?

Playwright is startled.

ACTRESS: . . . This? (*Another caress.*) Maybe this?

Playwright reaches for her hand as if to bring it to his lips, but she eases away.

ACTRESS: But Daddy, like I said: it wasn't anything actual, y'know?

PLAYWRIGHT: (*Agitated.*) "Actual" . . . ?

ACTRESS: Just something in his office? Like . . . a present to him? He asked to interview me. (*Pause, as if such an honor astonished her.*) He was skeptical, he said. *Why'd a famous movie star want to study at his theater?* He thought it was . . . some kind of publicity thing? Like anybody'd care where I went, what I did? Now I'm done with movies? (*Pause.*) He fired these questions at me. He was suspicious, I don't blame him. I guess I cried. (*Pause.*)

PLAYWRIGHT: What kind of questions did he ask you?

ACTRESS: My . . . motivation.

PLAYWRIGHT: Which was?

ACTRESS: (*Almost inaudibly.*) To ... not die.

PLAYWRIGHT: What?

ACTRESS: To not die. To keep on ...

PLAYWRIGHT: Was that when he touched you? To "comfort" you?

Actress is agitated and doesn't reply.

PLAYWRIGHT: Eventually he made love to you, yes? How many times?

ACTRESS: Oh, it wasn't l-love! I don't know ... Gee, Daddy, this makes me feel bad. You're mad at me.

PLAYWRIGHT: Darling, I'm not mad at you. I'm just trying to understand.

ACTRESS: I didn't even know you then! I was ... divorced.

PLAYWRIGHT: You always, unfailingly, met in that ... smelly ... office of his.

Actress shrugs.

PLAYWRIGHT: That greasy ... stained ... sofa of his.

Actress shrugs.

PLAYWRIGHT: Why?!

ACTRESS: I was so flattered! This New York intellectual ... this brilliant ... *Jew* ... So many books in his office! And he'd read them, you could tell. Some of them ... the titles I could see ... in German? Russian? A picture of Mr. Pearlman with Eugene O'Neill. All these great actors ... (*Excited, recounting.*) I saw this book in German? I'd read, in English? (*Mimes pulling a book off a shelf, opening it.*) Scho-pen-haur-er. I made this joke, "I can sure read Scho-pen-hauer better when he writes in English, than like this."

PLAYWRIGHT: (*Laughs.*) That's funny.

ACTRESS: (*Pleased.*) Mr. Pearlman laughed, too. (*Pause.*) But he didn't believe me, I'd read that book. In any language. (*Pause.*) I mean, I read some parts of that book. A photographer I used to know gave me a copy ... "This is the unsparing truth, *The World as Will and Idea.*"

PLAYWRIGHT: Bullshit! A woman like you, contaminating your mind with "philosophy."

ACTRESS: I read it till I felt too sad.

PLAYWRIGHT: (*As if conceding a point.*) He was always saying, people asked about you, how surprised he was. Your quality. What you're really like.

ACTRESS: (*Shy.*) Gosh, what'd that be? What I'm really like? (*Pause.*)

Playwright types a few words, staccato as if inspired.

ACTRESS: Oh, Daddy, you don't ever tell people, do you? Because I'm your ... wife.

Playwright continues typing.

ACTRESS: (*Anxious.*) A husband and a wife, that's a sacred bond. Even the law honors that. You can't be forced to testify.

PLAYWRIGHT: Darling, I would never speak of you. It would be like flaying my own skin.

ACTRESS: You would never write about me, either ... would you?

PLAYWRIGHT: (*Offended.*) Of course not.

ACTRESS: This that happened . . . with him . . . was just . . . just . . . what happened. How many times I tried to tell you, Daddy. Like a, a present to him, to thank him? Like . . . "The Blond Actress"? For a few minutes.

PLAYWRIGHT: You're saying you gave the Blond Actress to that pig. Let him make love to her.

ACTRESS: He wasn't a pig.

PLAYWRIGHT: He was a prince? A saint?

ACTRESS: How'd a saint make love? (*Giggles.*)

PLAYWRIGHT: Exactly what did he do?

ACTRESS: Oh, mainly just . . . kissing me. Different places.

PLAYWRIGHT: With your clothes on, or off?

ACTRESS: Mostly on. I don't know.

PLAYWRIGHT: *His* clothes?

ACTRESS: Daddy, I don't know! I didn't look.

PLAYWRIGHT: And did you have a . . . sexual response?

ACTRESS: Probably not. I don't, mostly . . . Except with somebody I love. Like you.

PLAYWRIGHT: Keep me out of this! This is about you and that pig.

ACTRESS: He wasn't a pig! Just a man.

PLAYWRIGHT: A man among men.

Actress moves away, restless; a touch of mania in her dance movements. She edges partly behind the scrim as if about to exit.

PLAYWRIGHT: (*Loudly.*) A man among the Blond Actress's men.

Actress returns, gliding in a dance routine.

ACTRESS: Now I remember! I'd think of how it wasn't me anyway. But Magda in your play. (*She's thrilled.*) The gift you were giving me, and I hadn't even met you . . . yet.

PLAYWRIGHT: He cast you without consulting me. He did all the casting when he directed.

ACTRESS: He didn't tell you about me, I know! I was so scared . . . I revered you so.

PLAYWRIGHT: He told me, "Trust me. I've got your Magda."

ACTRESS: Did you trust him?

PLAYWRIGHT: (*Has to admit this.*) Yes.

ACTRESS: Why I don't remember better, my m-mind gets stuck on a role I'm doing, and I . . . it's like I'm in two places at once? With other people but not . . . with them. Why I love to act. Even when I'm alone I'm *not*.

PLAYWRIGHT: Your gift is so natural, you don't "act." You require no technique. Yes, it's like a match being struck. A sudden flaring flame . . .

ACTRESS: (*Mild protest.*) But I like to read! I got good grades in school. I like to . . . think. It's like talking with somebody. In Hollywood, on the set, I'd have to hide my book if I was reading . . . (*Laughs.*) People thought I was strange.

PLAYWRIGHT: Your mind can get muddled. You're easily influenced.

ACTRESS: Only by people I trust.

PLAYWRIGHT: *I* trusted Pearlman.

ACTRESS: He never hurt you. He'd boast about *you.*

PLAYWRIGHT: When we were investigated by HUAC, Pearlman hired an expensive Harvard lawyer. Wasp. Me, I hired a guy right here in Manhattan, a friend. "Commie-lawyer," he was called. I was the idealist. Pearlman was the pragmatist. (*Pause.*) Damned lucky I didn't get sent to prison.

ACTRESS: Oh, Daddy! That won't ever happen again. It's 1956 now. We're more advanced.

PLAYWRIGHT: *He* had a sexual response, yes?

ACTRESS: Ask him. He's your friend from way back.

During Playwright's next lines, Actress exits swiftly.

PLAYWRIGHT: You and him . . . you never told the full truth, did you?

Actress has gone. Playwright glances around baffled.

Has the scene ended? Playwright is stunned. Goes to the window to open it, but it's stuck.

PLAYWRIGHT: (*Tugging at collar.*) So warm . . . (*Hand to forehead.*) Fever? (*Laughs.*) Then *I* can't be dead.

The Actress returns with several fresh-cut flowers and a vase with water in it. The flowers have large heads, like hydrangea.

ACTRESS: (*A manic gaiety.*) It's our anniversary, the day we *met.*

PLAYWRIGHT: Beautiful flowers . . . But you've cut the stems too short.

ACTRESS: (*A little sharp cry.*) Oh, again!

The Actress puts the flowers in the vase, but they look odd, with such short stems. She pushes the vase agitatedly away, and it would fall over, except the Playwright catches it.

ACTRESS: Why do I always do that! It looked . . . right.

The Playwright takes a shallow bowl, pours water from the vase into it, and floats the flower heads in it.

PLAYWRIGHT: You don't have to tell me, darling, if it's too painful.

ACTRESS: Tell . . . what?

PLAYWRIGHT: How many times . . . you and him.

ACTRESS: Daddy, I don't *know.* My mind's not . . . an adding machine. (*Pause, pointing at flowers.*) That's okay to do that, like that . . . ? Nobody'd laugh at you?

PLAYWRIGHT: (*Quiet vanity.*) Not at me.

ACTRESS: Not at you.

Actress is moving about restlessly. Lifts a leg, grips the ankle in an exercise routine.

ACTRESS: Funny, then, you'd have a wife. People'd laugh at.

PLAYWRIGHT: Why do you say that? Laugh at *you?*

ACTRESS: (*Hands beneath breasts, shakes herself.*) "Jell-O on springs."

PLAYWRIGHT: You invited laughter, you demeaned yourself.

ACTRESS: It's okay. If they can't have you, there's different ways of revenge. Men, I mean. (*Pause, dances.*) That movie I made where I danced, Jane Russell and me? We had to rehearse so much, all our toes bled. (*Pause.*) I loved Jane. We went to the same school, Van Nuys High, didja know that? We didn't know each other...Jane was so popular, and pretty. (*Pause.*) I'd get laughed at then. Guys would whistle and bang on their lockers.

PLAYWRIGHT: Remember, you said you wouldn't.

ACTRESS: "Dwell upon the past." Okay.

PLAYWRIGHT: We're alive *now.*

Pause. Actress giggles.

ACTRESS: We are? (*Dances teasingly away.*)

PLAYWRIGHT: Dancing is hard on the body. A body like yours.

ACTRESS: Just I started too late. You have to start young. Starve yourself...(*Pause.*) Why I was so grateful to Mr. Pearlman, giving me a new chance.

PLAYWRIGHT: (*Angry.*) The hell with that. I told you: you exaggerate his role in your life.

ACTRESS: (*Matter-of-fact.*) He accepted me as a student. Age twenty-nine. Offered me your play...*you* wouldn't have done. (*Pause; Playwright can't deny this.*) Oh, gosh, if he'd turned me away...that day...

PLAYWRIGHT: (*Quickly.*) Don't.

ACTRESS: (*Strange thrill.*) I'd think...if somebody sort of brushed up against me...on the subway platform...it wouldn't be my fault, if I fell?

PLAYWRIGHT: That didn't happen.

ACTRESS: (*Caressing body, laughs.*) BLOND ACTRESS FLAT-

TENED BY SUBWAY.

PLAYWRIGHT: (*Ignoring this.*) That's why you exaggerate. With him. You need to show gratitude. That's how you're "good."

ACTRESS: That's what it is? I guess.

PLAYWRIGHT: But this was before . . . you and I met.

ACTRESS: Oh, Daddy! Yes.

PLAYWRIGHT: And it was, how many times? Five, six? Fifty?

ACTRESS: What?

PLAYWRIGHT: You know what.

ACTRESS: Just four or five times . . . (*Pause, pleading.*) I'd go into Magda, I wasn't there.

PLAYWRIGHT: He was married.

ACTRESS: I guess.

PLAYWRIGHT: But hell, I was married, too. Yes?

Actress draws back guiltily.

PLAYWRIGHT: Did you ever . . . come?

ACTRESS: Huh?

PLAYWRIGHT: . . . have an orgasm? With him?

ACTRESS: You promised you wouldn't! Like this . . .

PLAYWRIGHT: It's just a clinical point.

ACTRESS: Why I wanted to die. Those times.

Playwright types furiously for a few seconds.

ACTRESS: Why didn't you let me, you bastard!

Playwright types.

ACTRESS: *You* wanted it, too. For me to die ...

PLAYWRIGHT: (*Reverting to his subject, as if he hadn't heard.*) Just tell me: did you ever have an orgasm with Pearlman.

ACTRESS: Did I ... oh, gee, Daddy, I didn't know you then, did I? I mean, as a real person ... (*Pause.*) I knew your work. I revered you ...

PLAYWRIGHT: Him "kissing" you. That mouth. (*Disgust.*)

ACTRESS: (*Agitated.*) Oh, gosh, if this was a, a ... script ... I'd know where it was going, and I w-wouldn't be scared ...

PLAYWRIGHT: Just improvise. Tell the truth for once.

ACTRESS: Oh, Daddy, if I did ever have a ... (*Pause, can't say the word.*) ... it was only just for that scene, you know? And then the scene was over.

Playwright yanks out sheet of paper, crumples it.

ACTRESS: Now you're mad at me? Don't you l-love me?

PLAYWRIGHT: (*Slowly.*) I ... love you.

ACTRESS: You don't! Not *me*.

PLAYWRIGHT: Yes. You.

ACTRESS: The Blond Actress, maybe. You loved her ... sometimes.

PLAYWRIGHT: (*More certain.*) Of course I love you, darling. I'd like to save you from yourself, is all. Wanting to hurt yourself.

Actress smiles and shakes her head vigorously, denying this.

PLAYWRIGHT: The low value you persist in placing on yourself.

ACTRESS: (*Excited.*) Oh, but, already I am . . . saved. By you. My new life with you. (*Pause.*) My *husband.* (*She seizes his hands to kiss them ecstatically.*) Your beautiful, strong hands . . .

A beat. Playwright eases his hands away from Actress. She stares at him searchingly, but he seems not to see her.

PLAYWRIGHT: (*To himself.*) It won't work. It's folly . . . It *will.* I can be strong enough for both.

A cue to Actress that the scene is ending. She backs away, dancer-like, twining a strand of hair around her fingers.

ACTRESS: (*Wistful, unaccusing.*) Daddy, you won't write about me, will you? Us talking like this. After I'm . . . (*Pause, awkward.*) When, maybe, you don't love me anymore?

PLAYWRIGHT: Darling, don't say such things. I'll always love you.

Actress retreats behind the scrim. Playwright can't follow.

PLAYWRIGHT: (*Anxiously.*) You know, darling . . . don't you?

Actress has vanished.

The Playwright tries again to open the window, but it's stuck. He returns to the typewriter, deep in concentration. With two fingers he types rapidly, a staccato burst of sound that ceases almost immediately.

Light fades on the Playwright and the bowl of flowers, which has been placed on the floor near his feet. Lights out.

Mondo Zapruder

*You know, there is this amazing thing that happens when you
begin to create a common history with someone. Each detail is
fascinating. You could just go to a mall and hang near the
fountain in the atrium, and you'll find yourself going over
that time as if it were the Zapruder film.*
—Mark Leyner

A Word from the Editor

Last month's issue of *Mondo Zapruder* sparked a flurry of cor-respondence among our subscribers (see below). When I
started this project over a year ago, it was my hope to stimulate
just this kind of earnest and impassioned discussion.

Our latest issue brings regular readers a twofold treat. First, I
am proud to announce that, as soon as sufficient funding is
arranged, *Mondo Zapruder* is going online. Our venture into elec-tronic media will greatly expand the print audience that has loyal-ly followed our progress during the last year. Subscribers will
soon be able to download frame-by-frame recreations of crucial
scenes from my inquiry, eliminating the need for hand-drawn
illustration panels.

I have saved my most exciting announcement for last: This
month's Postmortem feature at last uncovers the long-sought
Smoking Gun. Readers may view this announcement with skepti-cism, since I have trumpeted achieving this discovery in every
issue since *MZ* #1. But, as will be seen, the evidence contained
here is overwhelming.

My discovery should not be taken as a sign that this publication
has run its course. If anything, it will take significant additional
research and analysis to explore the ramifications of what we have
learned. Finding the Smoking Gun is only the beginning. Readers
can look forward to many more issues packed with the unique
brand of provocative editorial content they have come to expect
from *Mondo Zapruder.*

Letters to the Editor

Dear Sir,

Please do not leave any more copies of your publication in my newsstand section. As I have told you several times already, I am not interested in selling it. I have been patient with you so far, but if you disregard this letter, I will be forced to ask you to take your business elsewhere.

Salvador Montenegro
Proprietor
Sal's Discount Liquor

The Editor responds: Some readers may question the wisdom of printing such unfavorable correspondence in these pages. And yet I see Mr. Montenegro's resistance as an encouraging sign that free speech is alive and well in this country. Some people are not ready for the truths revealed in *Mondo Zapruder* (offered at the low, low price of $1.00 per issue, no less!). So be it. They are free to go elsewhere for the facts. I, meanwhile, am free to circulate my ideas among those more open-minded individuals who are ready for them.

Son,

Why must you waste your gift on what can only be called perversions? Don't you remember what the guidance counselor told us so long ago, how cinematic memory was extremely rare and yet to be fully understood? You had so much promise, so much potential for helping others. Remember Mrs. Halversen's class? You would do the most beautiful, letter-perfect recitations from "The Wasteland." It brought Mrs. Halversen to tears every time. She had never seen such an articulate fifth-grader.

What about in high school when you caught the vice principal molesting the Ferguson girl? You were the only person at the Homecoming dance who could remember seeing him drag her under the bleachers. The superintendent was so grateful for your testimony at the trial that he made you Good Citizen of the Year.

Now it's come to this? Publishing the intimate details of your life? For what purpose? Have you even bothered calling Dr. Kotzlowe? He is an expert on bereavement. I know he was a great source of strength for me after your father passed away. *That* was hard. What you are going through is nothing by comparison. Let it go.

And don't expect my help in getting your filth broadcast online.

Your mother

The Editor responds: It was "Prufrock," not "The Wasteland," and everyone was bored.

I was a witness for the prosecution because no one would dance with me.

There are many ways to lose and many ways to mourn.

Asshole,

Thanks for the latest issue. I was particularly amused by the skull and candy hearts that came with it. My lawyer, however, was not. Restraining orders exist for a reason.

I'm not the one with the cinematic memory, but your recreation of the last time we made love ("Postmortem," p. 5) contains several exaggerations and inaccuracies. I have never worn or owned underwear even remotely resembling what you have me wearing in panels 7 through 15. Also, I don't remember glowing so much after we finished. Panel 22 makes me look like a saint in a stained glass window.

Give it up. There is no Smoking Gun. People drift apart. There doesn't need to be a reason.

You know who

The Editor responds: Loyal readers of *Mondo Zapruder* will recognize the pungent prose stylings of my ex-girlfriend. For legal reasons, I cannot use her real name anywhere in this publication. Some readers, especially those with young children, were put off by previously used pseudonyms. After much thought, I eventually decided to refer to her simply by her first initial, B.

I am accused in B.'s letter of engaging in a fruitless, tiresome quest. But it is you, B., who are tiresome, with your legal maneuvering, your disingenuous denials, your stubborn refusal to see the truth. There are always reasons. Some of us are more determined to find them than others.

Of course, there is no better way to rebut the skeptics than to proceed to this month's feature article—

Postmortem: The Smoking Gun

Background

For most of the last year, I have focused on frames recollected from the Xavier Affair, a party hosted by David Xavier, one of B.'s colleagues from work. Readers will recall that this event appeared to be the watershed in my relationship with B. Her behavior that night was erratic, warm and jovial one moment, cool and distant the next. Though she rarely drank, during the 3.25 hours we were at Xavier's, she consumed two vodka martinis and one gin and tonic. A second gin and tonic was only half consumed when she decided that she wanted to leave.

On the way out, I asked her if something was wrong. She said it was nothing, maybe stress from work. As we approached her building, she loosened her grip on my right hand and began stroking my fingers in a quasi-clockwise fashion, a signal indicating that she wanted me to spend the night. This would be the last time we slept together.

Analysis of that night ran in our Valentine's Day double issue and revealed no new clues to the Smoking Gun, although it did bring to light several details of B.'s growing discontent. Afterwards, she turned away from me and slept the rest of the night on her left side. She usually preferred her right side, facing me, with her head resting on my upper arm at a roughly twenty-degree angle.

B. also kicked me in her sleep, an occurrence which, until that night, was unprecedented. In bed, B. would typically weave her legs together with mine in such a way that, on waking, I would feel neither numbness nor discomfort.

These days I sleep on the floor.

The Single Bullshit Theory

The following day, B. left a message on my answering machine in which she relayed her doubts about our future together. Repeated playing of the machine's microcassette indicated that the message was authentic.

In subsequent conversations, B. attempted to rationalize her decision to break things off. Two days after her initial message, she relayed, by phone, the substance of her so-called explanation. A complete transcript and analysis of this phone call appeared in *Mondo Zapruder #1*. A partial transcript is reprinted here:

> B.: It's not about you or anything you did or didn't do.
> *Mondo Zapruder:* Then what is it about?
> B: I don't know. It's about change. It's about needing more than someone who needs you.
> *MZ:* Is that all I was? Someone who needed you?
> B: No...not always. But now— What was that?
> *MZ:* What?
> B: That noise. That clicking.
> *MZ:* I didn't hear anything.
> B: Are you recording this?

My analysis of this exchange concluded that B.'s explanation was essentially bogus (see "Postmortem: The Single Bullshit Theory," *MZ #1*). By throwing around meaningless terms from popular psychology such as "needs," "change," and "growth," she was clearly trying to deflect scrutiny away from the central question.

Later, in person, I reminded B. of the serious consequences that would result if she was withholding evidence from my investigation. On hearing this, she became noticeably agitated, threatened to retain legal counsel, and abruptly cut off all communications.

Suspected Rivals Revisited

Undaunted, I began sorting through the available evidence. I did not do so naïvely. There are countless possible reasons behind the failure of a relationship. It was important to limit my search early on to the most likely reason for B.'s decision. The Romantic Rival Scenario quickly emerged as the best place to start.

The Romantic Rival Scenario was suggested in the first issue of *Mondo Zapruder* and remains the central focus of this investigation. (The Temporary Insanity Scenario and the Demonic Possession Scenario were proposed in *MZ #5*, but this was merely an editorial lark fueled by spring fever and cheap wine.) Simply put, I theorized that B. left to be with someone else. B. has repeatedly denied this allegation, and, to be fair, the evidence is inconclusive. However, there is much circumstantial evidence linking her to

David Xavier. This evidence has already been discussed in a special three-part series ("Postmortem: Suspected Rivals," *MZ #2–4*).

For various reasons, B.'s connections to Xavier called for particularly close scrutiny. As one of her colleagues, he had daily access to her both at the office and after work. B. never tired of quoting whatever bits of wisdom Xavier chose to share at the coffee machine. He had a vast repertoire of anecdotes from several different continents (he was well-traveled) and an equally vast list of books he recommended to friends (he was well-read). Whenever I would object to how much she raved about Xavier, B. would accuse me of being jealous. Readers know, of course, that I was never jealous of Xavier. I merely wanted B. to talk about something else.

As previously documented, B. informed me one night, before retiring to bed, that we had been invited to a party at Xavier's newly rented house. She watched for my reaction with an amused expression on her face. I looked up from the book I was reading and casually articulated my interest in finally meeting her esteemed coworker.

B. approached and stood next to where I lay reading. Promise me, she said, that you'll be on your best behavior. I responded with an indifferent shrug.

She slid the slender band from around her ponytail and let her hair fall loose around her neck. She knelt down onto the bed and straddled my lap with her bare legs. I could feel the fringe of her cotton nightshirt brush the tops of my thighs.

Please, she whispered, close enough to be heard.

I did not refuse her request.

The Mysterious Second Gap

The Xavier Affair initially seemed the likeliest source of the Smoking Gun, since it immediately preceded B.'s phone message and its aftermath. The early stages of this inquiry uncovered two potentially significant anomalies.

First, B. wore lip gloss that night. She almost never used makeup. She didn't need to, and I had told her this as we stood in my bathroom getting ready. She said nothing, gave me a small smile, and began applying the gloss to her lips. For the rest of the night,

I was distracted by the shimmery pink of her mouth and the soft fruit smell noticeable whenever she was nearby.

Second, I discovered a series of three time gaps in the Xavier frames. Each gap represented intervals of time in which B.'s whereabouts could not be accounted for. The first gap (G1) was fifteen minutes long; the second (G2) lasted twenty minutes; the third and final gap (G3) lasted twelve minutes. B. stated that at G1 and G3, she was in line for the bathroom. Eyewitness accounts corroborate her explanation. But, curiously, G2, the longest gap in the Xavier frames, has never been fully explained. When B. returned to the party, she said she had just stepped out for some air. However, this account has never been corroborated. In addition, David Xavier was reported missing from the party for a period of time that closely corresponds to the second gap. B. denied that there was any significance to this. Observations of Xavier's movements that night revealed him to be gregarious, quite handsome, and a good seven inches taller than myself. But, except for a brief conversation that I witnessed on arriving, there is no visual record of B. and Xavier spending any significant amount of time together.

In *Mondo Zapruder* #6, I reported the account of one witness who recalled seeing Xavier and B. share a marijuana cigarette on the steps of Xavier's back porch. This witness later recanted his story, saying that he could no longer remember if it was B. or he himself who had shared the cigarette with the host. Analysis of B.'s appearance and behavior in the minutes following G2 was inconclusive in supporting the witness's claims. She did not appear to be intoxicated. However, her apparent lucidity was marked by a subtle, yet noticeable air of guilty self-consciousness. When we spoke, she avoided direct eye contact and answered my questions with vague monosyllables. Repeated scrutiny of this evidence failed to definitively implicate Xavier or any other guest at the party.

The Crucial First Frame

Having run into a dead end with the Second Gap, I was at a loss for how to go forward. Eventually, I decided to set the Xavier Affair aside and work on other aspects of the search. These aspects involved the historical background leading up to B.'s answering machine message. Although this process delayed work on the Smoking Gun, it would eventually lead to my latest discovery.

One night, after proofreading articles for an upcoming issue, I went back to the Xavier frames. I had not considered them for months and did not know what I expected from still another viewing. Perhaps I thought that with fresh eyes, I would finally find something.

There has been little formal scientific study of cinematic recall, but I have determined that it is aided by the use of blank walls, of which there are several in my apartment. And so, as has been my custom for some time, I took my usual place on the floor, dimmed the lights, and waited for the first frame of my recollections to materialize on the wall's bare plaster.

My viewing revealed nothing new. Except for the puzzle presented by the Second Gap, there was still no definitive clue to the origins of B.'s sudden change. After several hours, I decided to stop. I returned to the first frame, for embarrassingly personal reasons. Despite my disavowals in previous issues, B. could be quite beautiful, particularly in profile. The lighting in the opening frames of the Xavier Affair was especially conducive to appreciating this feature of B.'s appearance. I had focused so narrowly on her profile that I had never bothered to observe the actual expression on her face. Revisiting the first frame many months later, I saw how her eyes were lowered as we walked through the door, how her mouth strained to smile in greeting. I had discovered something crucial: B. had been upset from the moment we arrived.

How could I have missed something so obvious? It was pointless to speculate. More important were the ramifications of this discovery. If the change in B.'s feelings was already occurring at the beginning of the Xavier Affair, it logically followed that the Smoking Gun could not have occurred there, but earlier in the Chronology.

The Restaurant, The Missing Foot

Eliminating Xavier's party as the primary subject of this inquiry was a significant step forward. At the same time, it raised a confounding new question: Where else could the Smoking Gun be?

Using a timeline compiled from earlier research, I worked backwards from the Xavier Affair, closely examining each moment spent with B. This was by no means a trivial exercise in nostalgia. I was searching for any anomalies in B.'s behavior, no matter how small, that would indicate the beginnings of her doubts about us. Isolating the critical moment in eight months of recollections would not be easy. Yet, perhaps inspired by recent progress, it did not take long for me to find my answer.

Two weeks and one day before B.'s phone call, we had dinner at The Biscuit Case, a popular downtown eatery. Nothing stood out about that night in my memory except for our high spirits. B. had just been promoted at work, and I had been hired to do security consulting for a local bank.

As readers well know, every relationship contains its share of habits and idiosyncrasies. Previous issues have already documented the quirks of my relationship with B. For the analysis at hand, I would like to highlight one quirk in particular: B.'s sensitive feet. She was fond of slipping off her shoes and rubbing the soles of her feet against nearby surfaces. In restaurants and other public venues where tables allowed discretion, she would often wedge a foot into one of my trouser cuffs and stroke my ankle for extended periods of time. If she had to get up for any reason during these times, whether to use the restroom or check her voicemail, she would invariably, on returning, restore her foot to where it had been, smile, and ask, "Did you miss me?" (See "Postmortem: The Early Dates," *Mondo Zapruder* #11.)

The latter detail is crucial as we revisit The Biscuit Case two weeks before the Xavier Affair and what followed. Approximately ten minutes after we sat down at our table, B., as expected, slipped off a shoe and began probing the area under the table with her foot. In Illustration Panels 1 and 2 (see attached), this action is evident from the slight shift of B.'s body from left to right. Twenty seconds later, she found one of my ankles and proceeded as described above. This moment is indicated in Panel 3 by her sly smile and a slight narrowing of her eyes suggestive of pleasure.

After the salad course, B. claimed that she had to check her messages at the office. She removed her foot from where it had been, replaced her shoe, and said she would be right back. By counting the number of frames that elapsed while she was gone, I have calculated the length of her absence at 4.75 minutes.

Panels 4 through 14 represent a composite visualization of the ten seconds that elapsed after B. returned. As can be seen, she sits down, places her napkin in her lap, and...nothing more. After fifteen seconds, it is I who must initiate conversation by asking her how things are at the office. Most significantly, her stance in the twenty seconds after she returns suggests no movement under the table. In fact, for the rest of the night, she will keep her feet to herself.

Armed with this new evidence, I immediately called B. for comment. A transcript of my telephone interview follows:

Mondo Zapruder: It all started at The Biscuit Case, didn't it?
B.: Who is this?
MZ: You know who.
B.: You've got to be kidding. It's three o'clock in the morning.
MZ: Just admit that this all started after something that happened at The Biscuit Case.
B.: You're pathetic. [*Hangs up.*]

I Am Not Pathetic

The Biscuit Case opened its doors in 1955 and has been a downtown favorite ever since. It specializes in classic American cuisine. I am quite partial to the meat loaf platter, followed by the apple pie à la mode. It is best known, of course, for its freshly baked biscuits, served as appetizers before every meal.

The atmosphere in The Biscuit Case is unremarkable yet highly significant to this inquiry. The restaurant's cleanliness and, above all, its excellent lighting have helped to produce recollections of astonishing sharpness and clarity. The crucial frames from that evening show irrefutable evidence of the turning point I have long pursued.

The Smoking Gun

What follows is a reconstruction of events in the minute immediately following B.'s return to our table. For purposes of clarity, I have designated the first frame of the sequence as No. 0001 and the final frame as No. 1215. Significant moments in this sequence are depicted in Illustration Panels 4 through 30.

Frames 0001–0064

B. sits down and returns her napkin to her lap.

Frames 0065–0329

The events of these fourteen seconds have already been described in part. At Frame 0128, B. reaches for the basket of biscuits situated to her left and my right. She selects one and places it on a small white plate provided by our waiter. At 0320, she replies with a terse "Fine" when I ask her how things are at work.

I generally dislike attaching too much significance to particular incidents and events. But few can ignore the striking moments between 0319 and 0322. For, at nearly the exact instant that B. utters her terse reply, she slices the biscuit in half. Despite her attempts to dissemble through polite conversation, her actions reveal her true feelings all too clearly.

Frames 0330–0549

B. takes a piece of biscuit, places it in her mouth, and begins to chew. She usually enjoys the appetizer course. In fact, she often fails to finish her entrée because she has filled up on appetizers. (For more on B.'s eating habits, see "B.'s Favorite Foods," *MZ* #16.)

Tonight, however, is different. She chews mechanically and swallows quickly, as if to get it over with (0440). She says nothing as she takes another piece of biscuit from her plate.

Frames 0550–0587

I ask B. if she is all right. She has been silent now for thirteen seconds. At 0552, my hand enters the frame from the lower left. My fingers aim for B.'s right hand, which clenches across from me in a pearly fist. I hesitate and wait for her to notice.

Frames 0588–0624

B. looks at me for the first time since her return to the table and asks, Why do you always have to know everything?

Frames 0625–0918

The waiter interrupts us. I order my usual. B. is having the chicken salad on pita bread. When she is asked if she wants anything more, she says no, thank you. B. looks up and smiles at the waiter.

Frames 0919–1011

I stare at B., who is still staring at the waiter. I begin to explain myself. You look upset, I say. You were on the phone for a while, and I was worried that something had happened.

Frames 1012–1030

You turn back and look down at the table. You do not touch your food.

Frames 1031–1214

The blankness of your face begins to shift. Your mouth forms a smile.

Frame 1215

You open your mouth to speak.

The Beginning

We have now seen the beginning of the end. But what began the beginning? Was it something as simple as seeing an attractive waiter? Did he remind B. of something she saw lacking in her own life?

Did it start while she was away? Was it something she heard

while on the phone? Did she even use the phone that night, or was that just an excuse she used to be alone?

There are witnesses, dozens of them, that I must interview. The restaurant staff could provide important additional information. The restaurant's patrons also should not be overlooked. The images from that night are sharp enough so that at least some of the other diners can be tracked down. Despite the efforts of a few naysayers, this inquiry is far from over.

Conclusion

Don't tell me there is no Smoking Gun. It is real, as real as these walls, this floor, this bed that dreams fitfully of the weight of two bodies.

I will continue my search. I will not be intimidated. There will always be new theories, new angles, new haystacks in which to dig for the needles in your words and movements.

And there will be time. As a great poet once said, There will be time, there will be time. Isn't that what you meant in the restaurant that night? Isn't that what you meant when you turned back, smiled, but not at me, and said that life is never fast enough at eighteen frames per second?

Ancient Winter

translated by Jonathan Galassi

Desire for your bright hands
in the half-shadow of the flame:
they smelled of oak and roses;
and death. Ancient winter.

The birds out foraging seed
were suddenly snow;
like our words.
A little sun, an angel's halo,
then mist: and the trees,
and us made of air in the morning.

Onset of Puberty

Ravager of lethargies and sorrows,
night; safeguard against silences,
the age of offhand sadnesses
re-buds.

And I see boys in me
still slender-hipped,
on the shells' slope turn
anxious at my changed voice.

Sorrow of Things I Don't Know

Choked with white and black roots,
cut by the waters, the earth
smells of ferment and worms.

Sorrow of things I don't know
is born in me: one death is not enough
if time and again now the sod
weighs its grass on my heart.

For My Human Smell

Infernos howl
in the murdered trees.
Summer sleeps in the virgin honey,
the lizard in its monster infancy.

For my human smell,
thanks to the angels' air,
to water, my celestial heart
in the cell's fertile dark.

Vectors: 45 Aphorisms and Ten-Second Essays

1.

It's so much easier to get further from home than nearer that all men become travelers.

2.

Of all the ways to avoid living, perfect discipline is the most admired.

3.

Idolaters of the great need to believe that what they love cannot fail them, adorers of camp, kitsch, trash that they cannot fail what they love.

4.
Say nothing as if it were news.

5.
Who breaks the thread, the one who pulls, the one who holds on?

6.
Despair says, *I cannot lift that weight.* Happiness says, *I do not have to.*

7.
What you give to a thief is stolen.

8.
Impatience is not wanting to understand that you don't understand.

9.
Greater than the temptations of beauty are those of method.

10.

Harder to laugh at the comedy if it's about you, harder to cry at the tragedy if it isn't.

11.

Patience is not very different from courage. It just takes longer.

12.

Even at the movies, we laugh together, we weep alone.

13.

I could explain, but then you would understand my explanation, not what I said.

14.

If the saints are perfect and unwavering we are excused from trying to imitate them. Also if they are not.

15.

Easy to criticize yourself, harder to agree with the criticism.

16.

Tragic hero, madman, addict, fatal lover. We exalt those who cannot escape their dreams because we cannot stay inside our own.

17.

Every life is allocated one hundred seconds of true genius. They might be enough, if we could just be sure which ones they were.

18.

Absence makes the heart grow fonder: then it is only distance that separates us.

19.

How much less difficult life is when you do not want anything from people. And yet you owe it to them to want something.

20.

Where I touch you lightly enough, there I am also touched.

21.

If we were really sure we were one of a kind, there would be no envy. My envy demeans both of us—no wonder it is the hardest sin to confess. It says I am not who I think I am unless I have what you have. It says that you are what you have, and I could have it.

22.

Laziness is the sin most willingly confessed to, since it implies talents greater than have yet appeared.

23.

If you reason far enough you will come to unreasonable conclusions.

24.

The one who hates you perfectly loves you.

25.

What you fear to believe, your children will believe.

26.

Of our first few years we remember nothing: experience only slowly gives us the power to be formed by experience. If this were not true, our characters would be completely determined by our infant hours of darkness, pain, and helplessness, and we would all be the same. For her first six months my daughter cried continuously, who knows why. Yet she is as happy and trusting and kind as if all that had never happened. It never did.

27.

The road not taken is the part of you not taking the road.

28.

We invent a great Loss to convince ourselves we have a beginning. But loss is a current: the coolness of one side of a wet finger held up, the faint hiss in your ears at midnight, water sliding over the dam at the back of your mind, memory unremembering itself.

29.

If I didn't spend so much time writing, I'd know a lot more. But I wouldn't know anything.

30.

The wounds you do not want to heal are you.

31.

When my friend does something stupid, he is just my friend doing something stupid. When I do something stupid, I have deeply betrayed myself.

32.

If I didn't have so much work to keep me from it, how would I know what I wanted to do?

33.

My deepest regrets, if I am honest, are not things I wish were otherwise, but things I wish I wish were otherwise.

34.

I lie so I do not have to trust you to believe.

35.

Opacity gives way. Transparency is the mystery.

36.

To me, the great divide is between the talkative and the quiet. Do they just say everything that's on their minds, even *before* it's on their minds? Sometimes I think I could just turn up my head like a Walkman so what's going on there could be heard by others. But there would still be a difference. For inside the head they are talking to people like them, and I am talking to someone like me: he is quiet and doesn't much like being talked at; he can't conceal how easily he gets bored.

37.

Anger has been ready to be angry.

38.

It's easier to agree on the future than the past.

39.

Only half of writing is saying what you mean. The other half is preventing people from reading what they expected you to mean.

40.

They gave me most who took most gladly of my love.

41.

Back then I wanted to be right about my estimate of my abilities. Now I want to be wrong.

42.

Time heals. By taking even more.

43.

Self-love, strange name. Since it feels neither like loving someone, nor like being loved.

44.

What I hope for is more hope.

45.

To feel an end is to discover that there had been a beginning. A parenthesis closes that we hadn't realized was open).

Blow Your House Down

So the question becomes—no offense—
are men wolves or are men slop?
Because my heart is definitely a pig.

Each boy sings like a halfwit alone in a barn:
Little pig heart, little pig heart,
let me in. Oh yes, those farm boys

let loose to form cities
have a way with words. My whiskered heart
breathes—it grunts

through what looks like two
rudimentary bullet holes. Its singing
won't win me any awards:

Yeah, yeah. Or you'll blow my fucking curlicue
tail off. Well, it's all the same to me.
Same little billy club,

same little manifest destiny
in their pants. So now my girlfriends,
the ones who think anger is like mud—

a bore and the enemy of nice
carpeting—now they sing too.
They sing like Ma and Pa

when the crops die.
They sing loudly, without much hope
and not a trace of syncopation: *What on earth,*

if that's what you're calling it
these days, did those boys do to you
to make you hate them,

each and every one of them,
especially the handsome ones
and the ones with smiles

like ice cream truck drivers?
They should know better
than to ask another girl how she feels

about the horse that falls asleep
whenever she tries to ride it.
Not by a sharp, black hair plucked out

of my chinny chin chin. By way of explanation
I get close enough to their faces
that they can smell the just swallowed

corn on my breath. I make them slightly
dislike me, and I say
Hate them?!

Can a jiggle-thighed heart
hate the slop that makes her fat? Can a
succulence hate the teeth that opened her?

Well. They look away then.
They pull back the chairs, roll up
the car windows, pull the hats over their ears.

Like it's time to go. Like some great mystery
that always bothered them
finally makes sense.

Patience Is a Virtue

When something irks you, let your anger build—
Don't spend it in a temporary snit.
Don't leave your smallest passion unfulfilled.

"Let bygones be bygones," say the weak-willed.
Ha! Watch where a bygone goes, and bottle it.
Appreciate your anger. Let it build

Vast *caves* of vintage rage, best when chilled.
Invest in every wrong and market it.
One's passion must not languish unfulfilled.

If Noah annoyed you while he hammered and drilled
His ark, stay calm. Wait till the varnish has set
To strike that match. Let your anger build.

Say the boss takes credit for work you billed,
Then wins an award. Act thrilled. *Wait.* Then quit
When he's sick. Don't leave passions unfulfilled.

Just keep your minefields mummed and daffodilled.
If someone dots your lawn with his dog's shit,
Lie low in it. Let your anger build.
Let your anger build. Let it build.

Heat Wave

The man had cornered a great deal of money and when it got
Hot he went—could go—where it was cool. As for
The servants, well, *tant pis.* A.C. was not yet part
Of the picture. But an icehouse. There you had it. The butler's

Gopher boy and an upstairs maid called Sophie (whose
Lonely duties were smoothing the sheets and emptying
Ashtrays) would traipse by separate paths beyond the dairy,
The carriage barn, and slip into an icehouse cool

Under pines, closing the door four inches thick behind them
(Latch falling to with a clunk) and clinch like godlings, hot
Enough to dimple the blocks they lay across, only
A scrim of moistened sawdust clinging to marbly thighs.

Hands and Psalms

A hand is the terminus of a human arm, thirty-six or more
connected bones and muscles, all designed for grasping

but that's not how it seems to many of us: the tourists on the lawn,
shielding their eyes against the glare, me, waving back
    as though I were visible,

the girl at the Burger King on the way to Baltimore
whose DNA had skipped the sequences for wrist and limb,

jumping straight to digit, opposable thumb, so her hands
grew directly from the unballed sockets of her shoulders.

You'd think hands could do so little stranded there above her ribcage,
but they swayed like living epaulettes and held their own
    wise counsel.

I want to write a poem of praise to the hands that do what they are told
is impossible and forbidden, that can smack

a person silly or spread like a balm above the angled limbs of grief
and draw the clear stream of disappointment out,

to the knuckles that wedge themselves between the baffled muscles
and unleash the memory of another hand that held too long

or squeezed too hard or not enough, and for the men who wanted me
(without consent) when I was seventeen,

when I wore my green T-shirt with a yellow number twenty-three
emblazoned on my breasts.

Put yourself in my hands, they said, with no *may I put my arm
around your shoulder,* no *may I stroke*

the endolateral surface of your thigh, and like Mary in her azure hood,
I was lifted bodily into heaven.

Here is a poem for the chain-link fence
at the back of a softball field in Van Nuys, California, and the hands
    that did exactly what they wanted.

Even now, I hear my father on his knees
among the slender wheat-like weeds, his yellow leather gloves

trying to pull out all the wildness. He says I'm going to hell
in a hand basket, and I wanted that, *didn't I, didn't I?*

Our Story

We hate the future in early fall.
You are worn and I am sorrow
if sorrow is a woman who cannot see.
Tell me our story. Were we perfect

at seventeen? Did we make love
in a hotel shower while someone
nearby knocked and pleaded into
the night? Did you visit New York

in mourning? Did we meet on a
train platform where men folded
newspapers and buildings leaned
together like lies? Was it like that?

Did we whisper while the elevator
went down? Did we leave our clothes
on a Cape Cod dune then remember
a low-flying plane? Did we marry

and move to a cottage by the sea?
So much of the story already told.
The dresses I wore; the expressions
you wore. Our pictures in a box

in the closet. Who could blame us
for refusing to write the rest? Somewhere
there will be trouble, somewhere
an unhappy ending. Inevitably, an ending.

from *Black Series*

I didn't want to only dream in black and white,
but when the colors came back
they frightened me, the reds I'd thought I craved, their technicolor
poisons shimmering, an errant lens, a gauzy burning
dress.

Smooth forms deceive,
give way to their own chaos. It seemed all equal signs
had fallen off the earth—
or was the earth singing equivalences
I couldn't catch?
I could feel the breaking webs, each vexed and battered
hesitance like wind, the crucial wreckage
of the cover stories flaring and dissolving like burnt footage,
daylilies opening, as in a dream of staying.
What is steady? What is not usurped?

In curious May I felt my mind become a place where filthy wings
of screech owls break apart, where dead twigs blossom
in the mud, where roots and stems are culled from riverbanks to harm
and sometimes heal, where bewildered trees awaken
and can't move, where slit necks drink in potions that renew
them, and questions prowl stream-like through the dirt
only to end at moss-covered rocks
that never answer.

I could feel the intertwinings as they moved in and out of me,
hurrying over my open eyes, my skin, as if I was watching
many films at once, and they were entering each other
as I watched, their colors swirling, blending in,
horizon lines collapsing,
voices breaking beneath the weight of many voices.

Once I lay in a white room, as if I wasn't born.
A plain unmutilated place beside the sea.
In the next room a couple held and kissed each other,
yellow loosestrife bright outside the window, then the stars.

Even This

At that time I didn't understand
snow, the absence inside July,
water and what holds the water
in. Heard "It takes more than a forest

to make a tree" in no one's voice. By then
the word meridian was extinct, echo
without a face to place it, make it
stay. Birds' theories of heat

hunch humid air
flat. Sparrows, finches, wrens,
and chickadees, their bodies
move too quickly through it

and exhaust their element: drop
like Coke cans and smoked-down cigarettes
beside the berm. Natter of bees
above new garbage cans

and wasps' happenstance
in chewed-paper air, fringe
of summer selves festooning
Halsted Street: I fall prey

to prey, a catch just the size
of my blind eye. The visual
is punctuated with interruptions,
handwritten paragraph of place

signing the bodies with sight
and mesh tank tops. Keep walking
and the lake finds you, keep walking
into teal strewn with fluorescent

orange lifeguards, random Adams
in rowboats and baggy trunks. Keep
walking, let bygods be bygods, Saint
Sisyphus, Saint Tantalus, Saint Ixion

of the Ferris wheel. Who could lift those fallen
concrete slabs flourished with boys'
unlikely chosen names? Cartouche
and petroglyph, etch and unetch: the lake

beards artificial rocks with blue
-green algae, names them
its own. Sunlight sticks to my skin, contagious
radio, fine sheath of heat and the beginning

of exposure: an immature ring-billed gull
run over by a biker, jogger, roller
-blader, then waved aside, papier-mâché
piecework shuffled into gray

retaining wall, shored-up cement reef
at Hollywood Beach with the rebars
pushing through the grain. We step around
it on our way to water which made us,

makes up our minds for us: no salt
but other minerals, lake absence
makes the shape of things.
And also in Arcadia.

Money Can't Fix It

My eyes must be open because light
through the woof of the hut's weave
shows my arm in pin shivers. What
wakes me?

   A howl unfolds outside,
fear-in-the-mouth, a breathing trill,
certifying the silence after. Sheep
in a barn as flimsy as mine

drum panic that my bones pick up,
an arthritis of fear. I stand, or at least
the dark and the sleep leave on another level,
   that kind of attention.

   My story is half-heard and resented
in a bar where A-7 has played fierce
as a drill since midnight, where now
someone breaks something

   and even the guy on my left
stops with his hands. When the cry comes,
there's this blip in the neon
   we all watch.

     Money can't fix it
says the jukebox, going on
while the glass gets swept.

Love Dies Hard

He returns her valentines
with the misspellings underlined.

Her life story read like a subpoena.
Her pen leaks in his pocket.
He wears the shirt for years.

His life reads like an instruction manual.
He wears red socks to her mother's funeral.
Her life story reads like a purchase order.

She memorizes the work of his rivals.
Their life story reads like a menu.
Their plates are scratched and gouged.
They wear knives and forks on their belts.

He burns her manuscript,
Their life reads like the Marine Corps manual.
Their bed is unmade and bloody.
They wear shoulder holsters under their bathrobes.

He reads his collected works into her answering machine.
She unwinds the spool.

Their life story reads like an itemized bill.
Their carry-on luggage waits by the door.
They wear their memories like faces.

They put the dog to sleep.

Titzone

Gyn's packaged in pastel. I'm in the pink
suite of X-Ray wrapped in baby blue
(opens-in-the-front) behind a pink-
flowered curtain, waiting for the pink-
and-white-clad tech. The dressing room's a cell
smaller than solitary, papered pink.
In the waiting room a fretful pink-
with-fever baby settles at the breast
of her mama. I reminisce: my breasts,
oozing comfort food, white sap from pink
papaveraceous pods. Mammary, thanks
for the memory. *—My turn now? Thanks.*

—First put this on. I'll tie it for you. —Thanks.
Lead aprons come in pale carnation pink?
—Now nipple markers. Right's a BB. —Thanks.
—Left's a wire. Some pasties, eh? —Uh, thanks.
The warden towers in silver and gray-blue.
—Left up first. Lean in. Here, let me. —Thanks.
—Now hold it. (Masher!) *You okay? —Yes, thanks.*
SWAT team gammas search me cell-to-cell.
It all begins and ends with one rogue cell,
then two, then four. *—All done!* The jaws part. *—Thanks.*
The salver pivots. I offer my right breast.
A glass-pressed face. Wincing? Leering? My breast!

They'll send a singing mammogram: Dear Breasts,
All Clear, or Uh-oh, either way, it's *Thanks.*
The tech is in her darkroom counting breasts.
She's left me with didactics: The Self-Breast
Exam. Six lumps from pea to kiwi, pink
plasticine, to demonstrate what breasts,
unchecked, can grow. And look, a practice breast,

wrecks the decor with clashing navy blue,
not from woad or dyer's broom, sweet blues,
but blue from midnight, ecchymotic breasts,
and the uniform who guards the holding cell
as Sunday invades Saturday, cell by cell.

First they take your shadows, then your cells.
Interrogated, you make a spotless breast
of it. My friend, you can't mistake those cells
(don't name them) wild-at-heart, renegade cells.
Remember our first training bra? (No thanks.)
It bound my torso tighter than a cell,
uplift and separation, cell-by-cell,
hooks-in-, eyes-on-me, vulcanized in pink.
(Where's the tech. It's cold in here. Fuck pink.)
What grace holds off the ambush in each cell?
Timor mortis begins with just one blue
note. That's all it takes to sing the blues,

ladies, sisters, cowled in black and blue.
But something's kindling in a weft of cells,
moonlight in a thicket, thin and blue,
as ghosts or milk or snowfall's hidden blue,
that makes my lips twitch. Rooting for a breast?
No, I'm just thirsty. Nothing that a blue-
stocking like myself can't take and blue-
ink into poems. *—I can leave now? Thanks.*
I settle into sunlight, giving thanks
for jet black, forest green, and cobalt blue,
crab pink, botryoides pink, sarcoma pink
(those dot-dash pasties chafed my nipples pink).

Once home I'll turn my back on pastel pinks,
and dial my spectrum up from powder blue
to ultraviolet, cell by cell by cell,
waiting for the telegram's Dear Breasts.

—Did you remember milk? My darling, thanks.

A Picture of Time

You say there's no time like the present. But what is the present here? I've watched TV for ages and seen movies since I was three. TV's daily life and movies are a communal fantasy. Today is in color, yesterday's in black and white, and there's no agreement about tomorrow.

I hear music everywhere, and then there are voices. Everyone's speaking in a flow and rush of language, the words are like water. There are echoes, too. And I know the whispering won't stop. It's the past. Time passes on and fools us by living underneath the surface.

You say there's a reality we all exist in, and I say I won't agree to it. You become red, enraged, and I make something from that. Red becomes an opening, surprising you. But I put it in the corners, where its brilliance is held in suspension. I keep explosive red, like time, to myself. I keep it, like dreams and wishes, for myself.

I suppose it's obvious. I'm always fighting time. It's relentless in its mission, and I'm nothing to it. But there's no time in dreams, which is why I need them. There's protracted suspense, the ragged drama of discontent and tempestuous wishes. And morose blue may suddenly pop up, disguised as threat, to announce the predatory present. I may be able to appease it, the blues, if I can find a place to put it. Even in dreams I want to control sadness and danger. I surround and contain them, and later everything catches up with me.

You say take hold of yourself. I hold on to dear, difficult life and keep track of success and failure—and loss, the holes and emptinesses where I could fall off and forget the world. Oases and shelters beckon, tempting illusions wrapped in bars and stripes. I reach them and take the time to think about what to do next.

Time moves on without my consent. I should have known better. My schemes might be planted next to startling green thoughts and in earthy, black fields. If I'm lucky, the dark is rich and compassionate and will let me rest for a while. Something good might come along.

Is it judgment I'm awaiting or mercy? I don't know. I draw a broad line around myself and make a fortress against inevitability. Suddenly there's static, an impish, contentious energy I never expect. It disrupts connections, compelling me to assimilate forces I don't fully comprehend. Like electricity, which I've never stopped relying upon. I know it was discovered and had to be captured, even subdued. Yet it was always there, and it probably wasn't waiting, the way I am.

You're naked, you say. Protect yourself. I cover myself in shame, lust, and greed, smearing and hiding the humiliating marks of battle. I've done this many times and have become a funny kind of palimpsest. You say no one can escape, and I run down a narrow, single-minded trail. I burrow deep and throw on another layer, for warmth or as a palliative. I grow big and orange. Fire is more orange than red and, like anger, throws off more heat than light. When it dies, there are embers and ash, wan reminders of its glory. The sky becomes night and swallows everything. The night is a thrilling action figure in the human theater. I hide in the dark.

You say I can't fight the inevitable. But what else is there to fight? I arrive at my destination and tremble at reason's door. It's inviting to enter, seductive, but there's really not enough room. Still I've learned I can't be an exception and walk in through the back door. To outfox reason's complacency, I escort the unpredictable unconscious. As usual no one notices. Later, perpetually, everyone's surprised.

You and I watch the current match between rationality and irrationality. I bet on what we can't know, which wrestles with everyone's limits and confounds certainty. It usually claims victory, and tonight I win easily. There was more behind the scenes than we ever appreciated. You're sorry to lose, and I console you. But the truth is I applaud the victory and prefer it to reason's insensible claims. Like the one that says time heals all wounds. Time's no cure, no doctor. You and I go on. We continue somehow, and our persistence is the source of everything we make. I want to surrender, but I can't, and I live in that paradox, and so do you.

Wild Life

The room was alive. I knew it better than my body. The whole house sighed and shuddered, breathing inaudibly through its doors and windows.

In and out, in and out I went, and one existence melted like snow into another. The sun was fierce and crazy. I cooled in green pools or under the shade of gracious trees. Beneath the stalwart moon, luminously impassive, I imagined the world. In my dreams, someone like me, a sprite, shimmered and danced, as dramatic as a noonday shadow. Day leaked into night, and going to bed was my first compromise.

Life spread itself before me, lay there like the backyard on a summer morning, the blacktop highway drifting out of town. I saw with my hands, envisioned with my skin, tasted with my eyes. At night the neighbors' houses shut their doors and lights, and I drew faces and pasted flowers and shells onto sheets of paper. I marked passing moments and kept mementoes, making sense of an immense unruliness. Even then I was captive, and it was uncapturable. So was I.

Laughter and fireworks, danger and whispering, skinned knees and fights delighted or stunned me, then metamorphosed into streaks of light and color, unstable images, and memory. All things had lives of their own, distinct from mine and part of mine, too. I was unformed, in a hurry, and always late. Time was the yellow school bus, waiting for me at the corner.

Intimations of death and freedom flirted and blinked knowingly. I lay on my back, conjuring tomorrow. The sky appeared to be my plate-glass window to heaven. I'd go there if I were good. The grass smelled fresh and warm, and I didn't want to leave the earth. I dug my toes in the dirt, startling ants that marched industriously across my naked stomach. Occasionally I glimpsed the future, which was a secret. I'd have a dog, a figure, a job, know bad boys, read bad books, stay up late. People said I was a girl with promise. Cross your heart and hope to die.

When anonymous breezes caressed me, I trembled, and when finally the wind stirred me, I didn't know its name was lust. Longing was spectral. At first I was a spectator, but I was destined to become one of desire's permanent guests. What was wanting? Every inexperienced day, I sought experience and swore allegiance to myself. I practiced no science, though patterns were everywhere. I thought I concocted my own.

Time didn't wait forever, and I took the train out of town. I didn't intend to go back. Unpracticed, I learned lyrics to old songs: Walls don't keep secrets. Roads end. Hope's necessary. Bridges collapse. Love starts and stops. Promises are made to be broken. Shaken, I settled, only to discover the dictatorship of the temporary. Longing and time were constant, though, and they were companions in ravishment. But the past never diminished and was not impoverished. Still, I tried to save it, enrich it, and, more beggar and thief than savior, returned to it again and again.

Crow

Thief of the corn, patch of night against a perfect sky,
I see you there watching me with your strange eyes.
     What message do you bring me?
When the leaves fall you'll be all we have left.
Perched above the cemetery walk, you add your two cents' worth
     when he reads the part about the promised resurrection,
neither curious nor afraid, and in that you are nothing like us.
How do you survive the winter?
When that dog snatched the meat from your mouth after
     it asked you to sing,
you chased after it, you didn't sing anyway.

Jonah, Going the Opposite Way

To Spain, and not a single day of awe there.
The Spanish swans lifting from the river: no ripples.
To sit in a spring whose waters offer no prophecy.

The not-expected. No one reading your mind.
No stopping the light inside the beast from crumbling.

Long ago, a fog came to settle on a low meadow.
And your old mare raising her head up to it
when it drifted down. That happy whinny
at the moment she disappeared.

A .   J .   V E R D E L L E

October, 1900

Summation:

It was deliberate.
We had to burn our barn,
let our harvest go.

Precipitations:

Mama lost the baby,
Father did not come back from town.
The chestnuts failed again.

We were distressed.
Particularly lost.
At winter's eager edge.

The Process:

We bemused ourselves.

Considerations:

We could not:
leave Mama alone with her cavernous
dry belly,
her grieving, stolid eyes.

Father and the farm required
our scissor-walking legs
and ever pumping arms.

We were used to use.

Decision:

To preserve ourselves,
resources,
we destroyed what could be
made again
and drank in piercing
sticky smoke
from charred and liquefying fruit.

LIZ WALDNER

Homeseeker's Paradise

road sign at the edge of town

A blue part that is remembered,
not a member of the class of prosthetic memories
but still a leg up,

a boost giving a glimpse over the wall of exile,
to a blue that is remarkable and lovely for a garbage can:
an aisle of blue garbage cans is what I see
when I look into the promised land.

Love was not a methodology practiced in Pisgah
which is the unfortunate name of the unfortunate town
in Mississippi where I was not born
but lived to wish I had not been.

Survival, witness, testimony—
these are the better part of squalor.

In Ohio, nobody at Riley Elementary
had seemed to notice what I tried to hide,
but the miserable citizens of Pisgah did:
the outward, visible sign (my existence)
of inward, essential disgrace.

For some garbage (I already knew)
a garbage can is too good a place.

The Present

R: A special present for my birthday?
How sweet of you. But what are you
thinking of?

T: Rather than some trinket,
beaded out of flashy stones, a living
gift.

R: A living gift! One that grows
on me?

T: Exactly. A present, out of all
our past, to keep you constant company.

R: Good! I'll never be lonely. Still
you haven't said what it's to be.

T: Bee's the word. Or words like bees.
I, plucking them out of the air,
will string them, humming, together.

R: Mmm, a present composed of music.
Sounds appealing. But dangerous too.
How, beyond their buzz, did bees
get into this?

T: Words, airier than bees,
thrumming side by side, also contrive
a honey-brimming hive.

R: With words
as airy as you say, how long assume
they'll cling to me?

T: As long as we
depend on breath.

R: That should be time
enough. But how long before they sting?

T: As long as you are sweet on me.

R: A fragile delicacy!

T: While it lasts,
this present lasts forever. Roused
by a breath—

R: Sleeping Beauty waking
to a kiss?—

T: in turn inspiring the breather,
such present presents an always present
present.

R: What riddlesome, knotted lingo
you resort to! I suppose it's meant
to bind your words.

T: Oh more's required:
stamped these words must be by clover fields
they've idled in, by winter bedding down,
by earthquakes, floods.

R: And, most of all,
by men and women storming through?

T: Indeed.
Words, so flavored, spread, a preserve,
over everything.

R: The world become one
savory dish! Are you not biting off
more than we can swallow?

T: I give you what,
honeycombed by your lips, you give me.

R: A present meant for two, celebrating
this life that we have lived together
more than fifty years.

T: A present made,
not only of the said,

R: but the unsaid.

T: As well as the unsayable.

Portrait Studies

May 24

A shake erupts, a self-guffaw.
Some miles up, he reads a life,
detailed with his own, by drugstore
specs on a wasp-boy's cord. His focus
is keen, a screen. Elated as he gets
in this fake air, the book's a scream.
Another shake. Across his aisle, two
toddlers shriek strange alphabets and wail;
his seatmate uncaps her dumpling pail;
he gnaws a thumb, then turns the page
and laughs, looks up from the book,
mimes my catching him *en flagrant*.
Unshaven still—last night luxe in Seoul,
he slept through the Headline Rant.

June 3

The place in which they were gathered
together was shaken—a Pentecostal
wind, that man, she said, and it may prove
true. Job rejecter, boot traverser—
too, the continent most populous—
œnologist (or œnomaniac-to-be?),
cigarified count on his island strolls,
nothing else admitted but me. Fuck that!

I'll bar the doors on his heavy bear
that lumbers gamely, half-asleep,
restless and shifting side to side,
turning on dimes to seal new lives,
moulting (by an insect's œno*cytes*)
sloffing and sluffing a path to me.

June 10

The inside of you red and raw,
The corpuscles at their work,
The churning of your heart.
The purpling of your privacies,
The smallest ridge behind an ear,
Your navel bud, your cowlicked part,
Your cheek plane flat, your iron
Calf from miles and years on wheels.
Your hair that curls on shoulder, chest,
Arm, thigh, your knee and hand—
The tags and moles, the set full lips,
The streaks of stretching skin—
Your starting dick, your furnace heart—
Please warm me, now, again.

June 15

WHAT SPOT? WHAT SHIRT? NO, THIS—THIS IS
MY BADGE MY GOLD BADGE IT'S THE GOLDNESS
SHIRT, I GOT IT FOR BEING GOOD. IT'S, SEE?
REMOVABLE, THE BADGE. NO IT ONLY SEEMS
TO RESEMBLE A PEPPER FLAKE, IT'S A SPY THING,
YOU WOULDN'T UNDERSTAND. THIS? IT THROWS
THEM OFF IF THEY'RE ON THE SCENT, IT'S SUPPOSED
TO LOOK LIKE SAND. BUT EACH OF THESE SPOTS
CONTAINS A DYE THAT WHEN RELEASED—LIKE THAT—
PREVENTS A SEE-ER'S FAST ESCAPE. NO, I'VE THE
SPECIAL RESISTOVICE—UNLIKE YOU, HAVEN'T YOU
WONDERED WHY YOU CAN'T LEAVE? ALTHOUGH
YOU'VE TRIED. I KNOW (US OPERATIVES DO). *NO!—*
YOU WOULD WASH AWAY THE SECRET FORMULAE??

June 22

Steamed. Harboring a grievous grudge.
Triggered by another's "helpfulness."
The face knits up. Scowl, hermetic seal.
Like the daughter in *Les noces rouges*
his do-gooder's only havoc wreaked,
and the spirit of it galls. Would that his
own insipid pleasing self not nip at his
own heels. It's the *simp*leness that irks,
the stupidity others manifest, pretending
selflessness. Contempt ties his brow;
a vice behind his cornea clamps down,
he stares off slit. Will such be all his days,
ignored while the dumb self-involved revolve
around themselves? *Helpful! Bull*— Scoff.

July 2

Late liquid light, and a swelled pool of it
dissolves the towers on the horizon south.
From within, the dinner done, he doth
survey the city's brim, swirl the liquid
in his cup, and drop his chin upon his palm.

Alas the sorrow of it all. He can recall
each false lead on repletion's lure and tweak
(the duplicity of each one stuns!); satiety
will not be duped, and craving will blaze on.

Across from him in her own fazed state, his
wife is not the balm. Lives he lived none now
will know—loves lost in the twining vines—
virtue's harvest rots in rows. So it (the sorrow)
goes, until exhaustion lays him down.

July 20

I TAKE THE PHONE. WHAT MAN IS THIS?
WHO WORRIES HER, NEEDING MY ADVICE.
NO METASTASIS, STILL LOCALIZED.
 I watch him nod and touch his toe,
 lean and listen to the other end,
 I see the question mark upon his face,
 hear *test results, if they can send*—
ONEROUS THE TASK BUT SUCH IS MINE—
FOR HER, HER FRIENDS, HER LIFE. FROM BRIS
I'VE KNOWN THE TISSUE'S KIND.
 Patience, authority, listening fast—
 and then, cell to cell from him to me,
 the outsize sacrifice of his nod,
 his burden of my relief.

August 23

Unexplained: Andy Capp is passed;
cartoon no more, the man is back.
Steadying a plank beneath his saw, or
tasting batter made for kings, even
arms splayed in a cutesy cupid's shrug—
the eyes work their lantern light again.

Now he's made a pile of kitchen crocks
—economy of effort's moved from
doldrums to what's light and quick—
and casts about for a packing box.

It is shop he's setting up, a house
he's cooked for love snug as—
the rug's in air, flapping clear, the
bug enwrapped in *him,* rapt dear.

from The Married Man

At the Boston airport they were separated. Julien had to go through the line for foreigners. He was carrying his big black artist's portfolio, five feet by three, zipped up. In it were plans for all his major architectural projects. He looked very respectable, if pale. Austin, of course, had been waved through Immigration, and he waited impatiently just on the other side for Julien before they went down to pick up their luggage.

To Austin's horror, Julien, whose English was still very approximate, was held at the Immigration desk for many long minutes. The stony-faced guard kept typing numbers or letters into his computer and studying the screen. He then asked Julien to step aside for a moment. Julien was smiling and nodding, even bowing, but he looked deadly pale. Another man in a business suit, tall, slightly balding, thin, finally appeared and led Julien into an office. There were no windows in the office; Austin couldn't see what was going on.

Peter's sister Meg had driven over in her station wagon to meet their plane. She was going to load up the back of her car with their things and drive them the fifty or sixty miles to Providence. Austin had met her just once. He went downstairs to the baggage room and piled high two carts with the duffel bags. He didn't touch Julien's luggage, since he thought he might have to identify his bags to the authorities. Maybe they'd mixed him up with someone else, a smuggler.

Austin worried that once he went past Customs he wouldn't be allowed back into the Immigration area, but he couldn't keep Meg waiting, either; she'd see from the Arrivals monitor that their plane had come in on time. As soon as he went through the last doors, which swung open automatically, Austin spotted Meg, a young woman as handsome as Peter but younger, less careworn. She was entirely healthy in appearance, the sort of sporty New England girl who looks uncomfortable in heels and as embarrassed as a boy in makeup. She wasn't masculine; there was even something fawnlike about her narrow face and big gray eyes; but she would have appeared more relaxed with a hockey stick in her hands than in her camel-hair coat with a black leather handbag dangling from her forearm.

Austin said, "I don't know what's happening. They're interrogating my friend Julien. You shouldn't hang around. We can always get a taxi."

"A taxi? That will cost you a hundred dollars!"

Six hundred francs, Austin thought. "That's okay. This could go on for hours."

"I'll stay here with you for a while, at least."

Austin thanked her. Shaking all over, he told himself to stay calm. Meg guarded his two carts and nine duffel bags while he went over to a Bureau de Change and cashed three one-hundred-dollar traveler's checks. He'd need money in any event. The people who were letting him their house had mailed him a map and the keys; he'd bought their car from them, sight unseen. Once he got there he'd have the car—

But what about Julien? He suddenly saw the balding man in the business suit hurrying along, and Austin rushed up to him. He explained that he was traveling with the Frenchman who was being retained. "What's wrong?"

"I'm not at liberty to say."

"Well, will he get through?"

"I can't tell you that."

"When will I know something? I left his baggage on the carousel."

"The luggage has been brought up to my office. It's safe."

"That young lady is waiting to drive us to Providence. What should I tell her?"

"She'd be best advised to leave. This could take some time."

"That means he will be coming on through in a few hours?" Austin raised his eyebrows and produced what he thought was a faint, ingratiating smile.

"No, it doesn't mean that at all. It doesn't mean anything."

"Can't you tell me what the problem is?"

"What is your relationship to the gentleman?"

"Friend."

"No, in that case no."

"Should I just wait here, then?"

"That's entirely up to you."

"Could you be so kind as to come back eventually, I mean after everything's been decided, and tell me what to expect?"

The man, who refused to return Austin's social smiles and seemed impervious to Austin's charm or even his quandary, looked at him coolly and said in French, "We'll see."

"*Merci infiniment*," Austin said. It seemed grotesque that two Americans in America were speaking French to each other. Did he think that Austin was really French? Was he, this official? Why wasn't he wearing a uniform? He looked like an Interpol agent.

Reluctantly, Meg glanced at her watch after an hour and said, "I've got to get home eventually and prepare dinner for my husband and kid. Dick…you remember Dick? He took the day off to look after the baby, but he's hopeless in the kitchen. Unless you need me?" Here she patted his arm in a psychiatric way, at once reassuring and distant. Austin felt sorry for her; she'd wanted to do a favor for the man who'd lived with her brother so many years. He knew that all the sisters had grown closer since they'd found out Peter had AIDS. Perhaps Meg had planned to discuss Peter's health with him. She was barely thirty, and she already had to accept the imminent death of her only brother, the only boy of the five children, this strangely unsuccessful, unmotivated, Europeanized problem in an otherwise hardworking American family (Meg was an award-winning kindergarten teacher with her own weekly educational television show in the Boston area; Alice had taken over her grandparents' pharmacy; Ellen banded migrating birds in a Tidewater reserve; Toni was a Chicago fabric wholesaler…).

But Meg's kindness, even her clearly indicated American "concern" in the way she knitted her unlined, silken brow to suggest how she felt for him, irritated Austin; irrationally he blamed her for "America's" rejection of his lover. Austin's heart was pounding, he'd soaked his way through his shirt, and he was caught up in alternating gusts of frenzy and lassitude. He'd start to gossip in a chummy way with Meg, then suddenly erupt in a panic over what was happening. "What do you think it could be?"

"Maybe there's something funny about his passport?"

"That's it!" Austin exclaimed, snapping his fingers. "Ethiopia!

He lived in Ethiopia, and these Boston goons are going bananas over the stamps. A spy! A bomb! Communism!" But then Austin immediately regretted what he'd just shouted; what if Interpol had highly sensitive directional microphones picking up everything he was saying? For their benefit he added, just in case, "Of course I'm joking. It must be something else."

At last Meg left. Austin was secretly relieved, because he feared that if and when Julien came out he'd be too shaken to make polite conversation with a stranger in English. Nor would he like to find Austin smiling and nodding while he, Julien, had been so anxious. More than once Julien had accused Austin of being more concerned about pleasing a stranger than loyally helping a friend—or his lover.

Eventually the announcement on the big board of the arrival of their plane was effaced. A popcorn machine somewhere (he couldn't see it) filled the warmed air with its distinctive movie-theater smell. A family of redheads, speaking with penetrating R-less Boston accents, was standing next to him. They looked as though they'd been dressed by Goodwill: the mother wore a dirty gray parka with a hood lined in orange quilting. Her black stretch trousers were covered with cat hairs, and her black boots had been bleached in patches by snow-melting salt. Her hair was flattened on the side where she must have slept. The older boy, dressed in a shirt stiff with dried orange juice, was coolly dribbling an imaginary basketball and, when their mother wasn't looking, quickly socking his little brother in the ribs. The little boy would start wailing each time. His face was filthy from crying and from rubbing snot over it. "Jason!" the mother shouted. Outside, through the plate-glass windows, he could see that night was falling rapidly. Car lights were pivoting as they turned through the thickening darkness and shone on the slushy road.

After two hours went by, the same balding man came up to Austin and said in French, "He's being sent back on the next plane to Paris at his expense. You can talk to him for ten minutes. Come with me." The man led him not through the baggage and Immigration section but by a back corridor; they had to stop three times while the man tapped a code into a lock and swiped his badge through a magnetic-band detector. At last they arrived at a higher floor and a hallway of plain metal doors and curtained windows. It seemed deserted. The only smell was of Lysol. A uniformed soldier armed with a rifle was stationed outside one door. The balding man unlocked the door and let Austin in. "I'll be back in ten minutes," he said.

"What a warm welcome America has extended," Austin said. Julien looked smaller and dirtier, his beard growing in quickly. They held hands for a moment, but Julien, looking around nervously for a concealed camera, drew away.

"What went wrong?" Austin asked.

"Our stupid lawyer didn't tell us that if you apply for a professional visa you can't come in on a tourist visa while you're waiting for it to come through. You really should demand your money back from that madman. You like people like that, you think they're funny, but look at the mess they've gotten us into. When I was going through the line they typed in my name and saw I'd applied for a professional visa. Thanks to your advice I was all dressed up as if for a job interview with my entire portfolio under my arm. If I'd had on shorts and a Hawaiian shirt they probably would have waved me through."

"When do you go back?"

"On the very next plane, which we have to pay for. It's the same plane we arrived on. It won't be ready till tonight."

"Can you pay with your credit card?" Austin had made him a partner on his American Express account.

"They'll accept the return ticket I already had."

"*Petit*, don't worry," Austin said. "I'll call my landlady and get my apartment back for a few days, and I'll fly back to Paris in a day or two. I'll call the president of the college here and get him to put pressure on our senator to hurry up your visa. Here, take this money." He gave him the two thousand francs he still had in his wallet. "Was that man difficult?"

"He made me speak in English for hours and then only at the end did he say something in perfect French. I think maybe he *is* French. The bastard..."

"Where will you go in Paris?"

"I'll stay with Christine," Julien said. Of course he had no choice, since he'd already sublet his apartment, but the words crossed Austin's mind, *I'll lose him to his wife.* He knew she had only a double bed and her couch wasn't long enough or stable enough to sleep on. In another week Julien would be learning his HIV test results. He'd given up his job, his wife, his apartment, his country and his language—maybe even his life—to follow Austin, but it hadn't worked out. "I'll call Christine to tell her you're on your way. She should be there tomorrow morning when you arrive."

"Tomorrow?—Oh. I'm so tired. Anyway, I have my own key."

"You do? To her apartment?"

"It was also *my* apartment. She never changed the locks. Why should she?"

The man came to the door. Austin stood up. "I'll call you tomorrow when you're back in Paris."

He had to load up his nine duffel bags in a taxi. Night had fallen, even though it was only four-thirty in the afternoon. The driver was a turbaned Sikh. Austin sat huddled up in a corner of the back seat, hating the Sikh and his loud voice as he shouted in his language into a mobile phone. He sounded furious, but from time to time, amazingly, he laughed, so apparently it was a pleasant conversation he was having with another Sikh. Austin tried to imagine the dog's dinner of dirty hair under the pomegranate-colored turban—they never cut their hair, did they? And how the hell did *he* get into the U.S. of A. with his dog's dinner hairdo and gold teeth, shouting away in his own language, when a well-dressed, well-behaved French architect was kept under armed guard and sent home over a technicality? They should never have applied for a professional visa. During all his years in France, Austin had been a tourist.

They were traveling on the very dark, forest-lined highway toward Providence at just fifty-five miles an hour, which seemed unbearably slow compared to French speeds. Luckily the Sikh's telephone signal had faded. Austin told him the story. The driver said, "Yes, Immigration is a bother. But don't lose faith."

"How did you get in?"

"My wife is American."

"How did you meet her? Was she a tourist in India?" Austin imagined a blond hippie.

"It was an arranged marriage. She's Sikh, too."

The highway, which had been dug ten feet lower than the surrounding town, wound gently through the outskirts of Providence. All the houses were of wood and looked huge. Despite their size they had almost no space between them, though he could scarcely see anything, so dimly lit were the streets. Here it was, just six or seven in the evening, and the streets were deserted. It was much colder than in Paris. The streets had been cleared of snow, which was piled high in banks on the sidewalks. Now they'd turned off the highway, and the driver was looking for someone he could ask directions from. But there was no one around. Presumably this was the downtown, but half the stores were boarded up. They went all around a three-block-long esplanade between unlit government buildings—Austin had forgotten Providence was the state capital. Someone had said Rhode Island was one of the poorest states in the union, but then again *Time* had ranked Providence as among the ten most livable cities in the country. The thought made Austin laugh ghoulishly. Finally they spotted a brightly lit chrome diner, or rather it was a take-out truck; several white teenagers were standing in front of it, blowing on their hands and stamping their feet against the cold. "We'll ask them," Austin said, but in a moment the car was surrounded by the kids, who were pounding on the roof.

"Lock the doors," the driver said.

"Go home, Towel Head." The Ayatollah had recently aroused American ire, Austin had read in the *Herald-Tribune*. When they drove off, the teens shouted, "Faggots!"

"Very nasty," the driver said.

At last a filling-station operator gave them directions, and they arrived at the proper address. The house belonged to the Professor of Aesthetics at the college; he and his wife were on a sabbatical in Italy. Austin's key worked. The Sikh helped him with the duffel bags. Austin paid him, and he left. "Cheerio," he said. "Best of very good luck with your friend."

The Story of the Deep Dark

In the cave, eons of time are marked in drops of water bled from stalactites. The old man guiding Phoebe is called Jean-Pierre. Short, hunched, bandy-legged, mostly toothless but still a smiler, he grabs Phoebe hard from behind, pulls her back into his chest, pointing with his penlight up into the cavern. There. Can you see? He traces the pointer of light back and forth. A bison head wells from the rock, an arched hump, nostrils, curving horns. Phoebe can see the chisel marks where a hand enhanced the natural sculpture of the walls, giving the bison a third dimension, a muscle that propels it out of the stone, out of its fifteen thousand years of stasis.

Formidable, eh? says Jean-Pierre.

At first Phoebe thought this was the power of the caves. The power to make still images move. Her own work is oddly similar. She runs a computerized graphics animator called a Harriet in a video house in San Francisco. The purpose of the Harriet is to transform her clients' products into things of magic. Cans of cat food into waltzing tunas. Aspirin into the soothing hands of a masseur. Cereal boxes into blooming jungles. The Harriet Suite is also dark and subterranean, lined with flickering banks of video monitors, twisted round the counter where Phoebe works with an electronic palette and stylus.

In the Musée National de la Préhistoire in Les Eyzies, Phoebe finds herself in a room filled with thirty-thousand-year-old carvings of female genitalia, wall after wall of rock lifted from the caves, imprinted with the cuneiform wedges of labia and vaginas. She's fascinated by these female forms, so forbidden, so forgotten, here gloriously afloat on the stone like fossilized confetti. The geometry is simple: triangles for the groin, partially bisected by the short lines of the vulvae. Phoebe is struck by the artists' clear familiarity with the subject, the minimalist renditions. *Compris-*

ing the earliest known engravings from the Western world, the museum caption says.

Once she had an argument with Vladimir, her live-in boyfriend, over a documentary on pornography she was doing pro bono work for. The filmmakers were lesbians who held the view that women needed to take over the business of pornography because only then they would have true control over men, emotionally and financially. Vladimir had thought this idea was bullshit. Phoebe had defended it more vigorously than she might have if Vladimir had agreed with it. Why do women want control over men? Vladimir said. Isn't that what they're so angry about in reverse? Because men live in a hierarchical system, shouted Phoebe. It's all they understand. If they're not on the top, then they must be on the bottom.

Their fight had resolved itself where most did, in the bedroom, Phoebe sweating, Vladimir grunting, their anger transformed into the carnal friction that defeats all the words and all the reason of the modern brain.

They've been planning this trip to France for eighteen months, since shortly after they met. Vladimir is an online video editor who works at the rival video house to Phoebe's in San Francisco. He's Lithuanian, dark, tall, with black ringletted hair that he wears pulled back off his face in a ponytail. Phoebe first saw him at her company's Christmas party in a rented Nob Hill mansion. He was in black tie, she in black velvet. They talked technical together over champagne: CMXs, ADOs, DVEs, Auroras, Avids, Harriets, Henrys—then left the party together for Julie's Supper Club, to dance.

Now she's come to France alone, at the last minute, their most recent fight proving unresolvable. Vladimir wants children. Phoebe doesn't. Vladimir can wait, but Phoebe, at forty-one, can't. Vladimir thinks children are natural, important, fulfilling, the perfect culmination of love. Phoebe imagines sleep deprivation, self-deprivation, fun deprivation, sex deprivation. She pictures getting large and giving birth through a small orifice. In the end, Vladimir thinks, women without children are slightly pathetic. Well, fuck you, said Phoebe, because women are no longer just walking uteruses for men's fantasies about potency.

The last exhibit in the Musée National de la Préhistoire in Les Eyzies is of the Venus of Laussel, a twenty-thousand-year-old bas-relief of a nude female, long-haired, with pendulous breasts hanging to her waist, huge fatty hips, and a bulbous belly. In her right hand she holds a bison horn, *The earliest horn-of-plenty?* the museum's caption wonders. *Perhaps related to fertility?*

Once during a warm September spell when Phoebe was crammed into her workstation by an unusually large contingent of advertising people, the air-conditioning failed, then the computers, too, wiping Phoebe's work away in a flash of darkness. The sports car she'd transformed into a white wolf during its race along a coastal road disappeared. The vectorscopes and color wheels dissolved into gray static. Three tense hours followed during which the technicians tried to retrieve her work. The advertising people swilled coffee and paced in the atrium. Phoebe called Vladimir from the telephone in the company kitchen, confiding her secret hope—that the Harriet would keep her images locked in its dark memory and never let them out again.

In the cave of Lascaux II (the original was closed thirty years ago), Phoebe studies—she's assured—a perfect reproduction of Ice Age art. The walls are filled with vibrant images of long dead animals. Black bulls, red deer, yellow horses, falling cows, fanciful unicorns, bison, ibex. But Phoebe finds it impossible to marvel at pigments applied in 1980. The only wonder for her at Lascaux II is the knowledge that there's still a Lascaux I, buried, not dead, but *unborn again,* its dark paintings smoldering with the life that Phoebe knows burns brightest in the absence of light.

During the third week of her vacation, Phoebe takes a picnic to the banks of the Vézère, under the looming cliff of the Roque Saint-Christophe. The limestone scarp stretches half a mile along the river. Scores of black caves riddle its face. A dark incision runs its length, a massive natural ledge cut deep into the cliff. She visited the Roque a week earlier, wandered up its terraces, its hand-cut rock stairways, poked deep into its caves. She saw where Neanderthals lived in the caves seventy thousand years ago, where Cro-Magnon moved in forty-two thousand years later.

But this afternoon Phoebe comes simply to sit in the cool grass between the river and the cliff, to drink a bottle of wine, feel the sun, listen to the lowing of cows. A thin stream of cars and bicycles winds its way under the cliff. Tiny figures ascend the five terraces. Snatches of lectures from tour guides drift down to her in a collage of languages.

If she were thirty years old, Vladimir could flatter her into pregnancy. But now she finds herself defensive of her gains, her time, her money, her professional status. She pours the black Cahors wine into a jelly-jar glass, savors its sweaty scent. She does wonder about old age, about the possibility of being alone. But is it really worth trading away what she has now? Yet, realistically, there's little hope of saving what she has now, though she desperately wants to. Without children, Vladimir will eventually leave her.

A bicyclist stops on the road, pegs one leg down for support. Phoebe watches him dismount, dig through his saddle pack, pull out a camera, duck between two strands of barbed wire, and walk across the fields. Phoebe sips the wine. He turns to focus, and she can see that the cliff is too large to fit into his frame. The next time he turns, he sees Phoebe.

Would she take his photograph?

Of course.

Here? With the Roque in the background?

He's older than her, with the wiry physique of a runner.

Phoebe lines him up in the extreme left corner of the foreground, dwarfing him beside the megalith of the cliff. She snaps the shutter, smiles, hands him back the camera.

Thank you, he says, sizing her up. Are you English?

American, says Phoebe. And you?

Parisian.

San Francisco, says Phoebe.

Okay, he says. My favorite city besides Paris.

Phoebe smiles. She finds that the French aren't sure about Americans, but San Franciscans, somehow, are wonderful.

This is my third trip through the Dordogne, he says. This is my favorite part of France.

Me, too, says Phoebe.

Your third trip?

No. Sorry. My favorite place in France. This is only my first trip.

She offers him wine, pours it into the second jelly-jar glass she'd brought (why had she done that?). They stand together, looking up at the Roque. His name is Jacques. He works for Peugot, but his passion is cycling. He loves this region because of the unique scenery, the sunken valleys, the towering cliffs, the startling castles astride every bend of the river. He's less interested in the caves. Too dark, too cold. He craves the sunlight after Paris. He loves the big oak and chestnut trees, the meadows, the black shine of the rivers. Jacques wonders if Phoebe is traveling alone. Yes.

That's unusual.

Perhaps not so much anymore.

And Jacques, is he alone?

Yes, yes. He always takes one vacation alone every year.

Is Jacques married?

Divorced.

Children? Yes, he's embarrassed to admit, six. Six? Ridiculous, he knows, but he was young, and had two wives.

Is he close to his children?

Of course. They're wonderful children. The eldest almost thirty.

He goes back to his bicycle to fetch a little walnut cake he'd bought from a farm near Périgeux. It's a specialty of the region. He breaks off a piece and hands it to Phoebe.

She tells him about the Harriet, her work. She confides her idea about animating a scene of Ice Age cave art. A pair of woolly mammoths, appearing in the video darkness as they might have appeared by firelight in the caves.

But you would never see the artists, she says. Only their work, appearing on the walls as if you yourself were putting it there.

Jacques thinks it's a wonderful idea, quite unique.

If you don't mind me asking, says Phoebe, but are you absolutely happy having had children? She struggles with the nuance of this question in French as she refills Jacques's wineglass.

Well, now, says Jacques. Of course I love my children. But to be completely honest, in a way, they were very hard on both my marriages, and they left me having to work all the time. Only now can I get any time back for myself. To bicycle, to see France.

Did you want children, or did your wives?

With my first wife, we were young, we both wanted to be parents. With my second wife, she was younger than me, and she wanted them. Me, not so much.

But you agreed to it?

Yes. Of course. I did not feel I could deny that to a woman. It is part of the contract of marriage, *n'est-ce pas?*

The sun slides into their eyes.

Were you planning to visit the Roque? Phoebe asks. Yes, says Jacques, and her? No, says Phoebe, she's seen it last week. Too bad, says Jacques. Phoebe gives him a wedge of her *cabecou* cheese wrapped in a piece of newspaper, and he gives her a hunk of his walnut cake. They wish each other well.

The first time Vladimir visited Phoebe at work he'd skulked into her video house, sheepish as a corporate spy. She'd pulled his chair next to hers in the dusk of the Harriet Suite, run him through her video portfolio, the clips of unicorns bursting into life, of dancing teapots, of fish turning into parrots. Vladimir had nudged her out of her chair, taken up her electronic stylus, drawn her a video picture of a stick man with a stick penis running toward a stick woman with balloon breasts. Underneath he wrote: The Lithuanian Chases the Bird in Pursuit of Love.

In the cave of Font de Gaume, Phoebe begins to cry. She's the lone outsider in a tour group of elderly English people. A tiny woman standing next to her digs through her purse and hands Phoebe a tissue. It is lovely, isn't it, dearie? she says, standing alongside Phoebe and studying the painting of the reindeer. For years, says Madame Binet, their tour guide, this was believed to be a painting of a battle between two reindeer. But now we realize it is a picture of the lovemaking of two reindeer. She waves her flashlight over the contours of the animals. Here, you can see how the male is leaning over the female. And here, if you look closely, you can see how he is licking the female's forehead. It is not a fierce scene at all, she says. But one of the utmost tenderness.

Four days before Phoebe left for France, Vladimir impulsively signed up for a kayaking trip down the Kobuk River in central

Alaska. Vladimir had never even been camping. His vacations tended towards quaint inns in pastoral countrysides. He looked defiant when he'd announced the trip to Phoebe, Phoebe leaning against the kitchen counter sipping vodka. He'd pulled himself up tall, tilted back his head. Phoebe recognized the posture: Vladimir, reclaiming his manhood. Well, shit, she thought, go ahead and throw spears for all I care.

He drove her to the airport for the trip to France, walked her as far as the security gate, where they'd parted, Phoebe tearfully, then Vladimir, too, the two of them clinging and sputtering. Phoebe had felt depressed the entire flight, had sunk into her seat, using three small bottles of airline wine to ease her into a boneless stupor. The last time she'd talked with Vladimir was by phone from the Gare d'Austerlitz, where she was waiting for her train to Bordeaux. She tried to joke: maybe we could invent virtual reality children, you know, ones you could turn on and turn off at will. Vladimir had grunted. We'll work it out, she promised. But when they hung up she knew that they were both wondering, How?

Phoebe's tour guide in the Grottes de Gargas is Yves, a French art student from the Sorbonne who's spending the summer working on the Ice Age paintings of the Pyrénées. Few tourists make it this far south, and Yves, excited at his audience of one, is going to demonstrate for Phoebe how the paintings were made. He pinches bits of powdered pigments from the little clay bowls at his feet, stuffs them into his mouth, chews until a blood-red foam seeps from between his lips. He puts a hand up to the wall, leans in close, sprays the paint in bursts from his mouth. When he takes his hand away there's a perfect stencil on the wall. He smiles: Would you like to try?

Phoebe chews, the two of them standing together in the chill cave. Yves leans in close, watching. You must chew until it's a thin paste, he says. Phoebe smiles, shakes her head: it isn't ready yet. Yves looks sympathetic. The taste is not too terrible, no? Phoebe shakes her head again. Actually she likes the metallic twang of the minerals, the sensory connection with them. She lays her hand on the cold cave wall, feels the warm spray of paint from her mouth. Her print, when she takes her hand away, looks small, the fingers curved outward.

Yves takes her into the main cavern, runs his flashlight across the ceiling until he finds a print directly overhead. Here, he whispers, you can see how badly mutilated this one is. His spotlight hovers over a twenty-thousand-year-old hand, the upper joints of all four fingers clearly missing. Jesus, says Phoebe. And this one, says Yves, is missing the upper two-thirds of all four fingers. Jesus Christ, says Phoebe. And here, says Yves, is one missing three fingers.

Is it just a few hands? Phoebe wonders. You know, the same ones over and over again?

No, says Yves, the prints are of hundreds of different hands. And they're not just folding their fingers down. Here you can see where the amputation is made between the joints. And here, the scar is misshapen.

What's that? asks Phoebe, squinting up into the light.

Yves moves his flashlight backwards a few inches. These are the handprints of children, he says. And over here—he flips the light over to the opposite wall—are the hands of very small babies. Phoebe studies the prints, the tiny, perfectly intact fingers stenciled in black and red, foreshadowing their own long-extinct pain.

On her last evening in the Dordogne, Phoebe strolls along the banks of the Vézère. The river eddies around the submerged tips of willow branches. Caravans of holiday canoes spin inexpertly downstream. Phoebe admires the grace of the landscape, the small motions and unhurried pace. Vladimir would love it. Would lie back in the grass on the banks of the river as she played with his hair and told him her idea for the Harriet. How firelight would appear on the mottled brown and white limestone of a cave wall, the torch itself unseen, but red flashes from the flames washing through, highlighting the stumps of old stalactites, casting deep shadows into the hollows. Then a fine splatter-pattern of black would emerge, growing into a sinuous line around a natural bulge in the wall. A second line would appear, around a second, rounder bulge. A third line would connect the two.

Three lines—magic—two mammoths. Long trunks curled around each other, tusks intertwined, humped shoulders flowing into shaggy backs.

She meanders up the winding road to the row of ancient houses built into the base of the cliffs in Les Eyzies-de-Tayac. Honey-colored stones glow in the last sunshine. Lights burn behind lace curtains. Phoebe listens to family-talk spilling out the open windows. Watches young girls setting dinner tables. Smells the perfume of black truffles and onions. She envies the clan warmth, the affection. In her mind, she begins to plan a new phase to her cave-art animation on the Harriet. The black-and-red splatter pattern will emerge in the mottled firelight, but as quickly as it appears it will begin to disappear, to erode grain by grain until only a faint outline of the two mammoths remains, trunks entwined, a suggestion, then nothing.

She walks past the houses, up to the next terrace. She gazes down over the gauzy darkness sifting into the valley. In Cro-Magnon times the caves would have been lit with the small flickers of campfires. Threads of smoke would have spun up to the stars. Ice Age tigers would have roared. She'd be eating reindeer meat, a Cro-Magnon baby curled into her hair. She felt the yearning for it, the neediness, but also the weight. Her breasts were big as watermelons. The baby was hooked up to them. Phoebe is pounding marrow out of bison bones. Where is Vladimir? Making cave paintings, she's sure, while she stokes the fire, tossing stones at hungry bears, her own dreams deferred.

Nothing has changed. Nothing would change. She has always in a way lived without him, since the beginning.

The Glance

Distance, detachment,
then, like lenses clicking

together at last in alignment,
the socketing, sprocketing,

then always, like flame
in a cave, sympathy first,

then perhaps fear, perhaps
for no reason something

like rage but always
this desire to parse, scan,

solve, these sensitive bits
of cosmos streaming

towards me like filings
to magnets, one then another,

no longer question nor
quandary, flown only,

only flown fleeting past
like waste light yet

not wasted, not sundered
or squandered, singular rather,

sacred, each with its own
awareness, each taken

for its time and taking
and let go, relinquished,

yet still held in its instant:
not waste light, *light*!

Scarecrow

Last summer the Better Boys bloomed,
tiny saffron flowers going off like slow
Chinese rockets, and set their pinhead fruits.
I'd ordered a pint of ladybugs from Burpee's
catalogue and scattered their crimson clock-backs
through the furry, pungent leaves. I sat
in my resin chair, observing the light
of late afternoons move through rinsed branches.
Back-capped chickadees
slurred whistled E-notes and dove—
an abrupt hop and slip with safflower seeds
into the weeping willow.
Love apples, nightshades, *lycopersicon*
esculentum. I read their poisonous
New World histories, studied the preferences
for powdered lime and a weekly inch of rain
(one drenched season I watched ripening
crack into rheumy weeping).
I could not act against the birds,
who love the bright cardinal red
of Fireball skins, the wet mass
of seed encased in a cartwheel
of pulpy gelled flesh.
                              I drove a stake
into the soil and wrapped the salt
marsh hay into my clothes. I made
the chest deeper, the arms more full
than mine, and stood him up at the shade end.
For eyes he had sunglasses, for ears sacking.
His fingers were my gloves.
I grew to enjoy his solitude.
Out there in the dark and light,
he never dreamed of what he was up to,

never had a thought
he didn't need. And when he came,
at last, to have a certain allure
to the thrushes and the jays,
I didn't give up, as some might,
on his stationary potentials.
Stranger things have failed to happen.
This summer a tornado two hundred
yards wide dropped a pine-framed tin garage
into our neighbor's yard, poised
to consume our house, and then
just rose over the roof and flew away.
I heard a Midwest couple on a talk show
tell how they rose into the funnel
saying goodbye. The husband said
he felt light through his closed eyes
the way a sleeper feels the dawn,
and he looked to see himself riding
"a magic carpet of air, skimming
over buildings at a good clip" until
God set him down ten feet away
from his wife on the ground, unhurt
till he sat up and got back-smashed
by a timber, breaking every rib.
They were happier now, each day
a sweetness. Yes; exactly. A sweetness.
Rooted like the smell of grass and lime.
The next morning I remembered dreaming
I placed a millet seed in someone's mouth.
Nights got longer, the scarecrow frayed;
scraps of his moldering entrails doubtless
lined the thrashers' nest. He never had
any sort of hat, so with glasses on he started
to look like the skinny blind man
who used to lean against the granite wall
of a bank across from the subway station.
I stopped weeding: the vines grew
freckled with liver-colored mold, turned
yellow as the flowers, and browned.

Still he stood guarding cages, until
my affection for him—like heat
from the earth's dirt skin—finishing waning.
I confess my relief at his uselessness.
I dragged him, one Indian summer day,
and all the tattered papery leaf-litter
he overlooked in mocking silence, out of that
manicured plot and down to the curb,
pocketing my shades and gloves.
I went inside and laid a pointless fire.
We weren't here when the tornado
lifted. We saw it from the freeway.
I was bringing my wife home
to Tuscaloosa from the Atlanta airport.
She was driving because she gets carsick.
I looked out my window and we stopped
under an overpass. The funnel was black
but its edges were glittering like dust
made out of glass, and the sight of it
flattened the sky. Out west, her nephew
was dying from stage IV neuroblastoma.
I'd stayed home to feed the cats and the turtle.
After I didn't light the fire I went out
on second thought to unbutton
my old white shirt from the scarecrow.
I thought I'd snip it into rags
and wax the cars. Instead I packed
some more books to carry over
to my new apartment. The moon
was orange and huge when I came in
to pick her up. Five miles up inside
the sky, she must have
watched the moon as she flew.
The birds were here first, my wife said.
I drove dead east, watching
little but my hands on the wheel.

ABOUT PAUL MULDOON

A Profile by Sven Birkerts

I first heard of Paul Muldoon through the affectionate enthusing of Seamus Heaney, who donned his conspiratorial mien—as if agents of some imagined opposition might be lurking near—and confided that his somewhat younger compatriot was "the real thing." I sought the work out, though I'll confess I was some time coming to it. This would have been in the mid-1980's, the time of *Quoof* and earlier collections. Accustomed to the solid subject-focused work of Heaney, who had taught Muldoon as an undergraduate, I thought Muldoon was working a bit too hard at the "Musee des Beaux Arts" thing, enthroning obliquity. But eventually, I made my connection. I readjusted whatever lenses I use to read poetry, and then, suddenly, they did not seem oblique at all. They seemed right, and much of the work of others, through that peculiar inversion of readerly tastes, now came across as lumberingly obvious.

Born in County Armagh, Northern Ireland, in 1951, Muldoon grew up in a house without many books. "Believe it or not," he writes, responding to my question about literary influence, "the only reading material we had in the house was *The Junior World Encyclopaedia,* which I read and reread as a child. Other books must have come from the local lending library...But the *Encyclopaedia* was my text of texts." The critic is tempted to take this cue and run with it, to find here the very source of the jackdaw-building principles of the poems, which, especially in more recent years, can scarcely curb their lore-braiding. On top of everything else, Muldoon is, in his poems, a retriever of the golden fact, a breaker-open of the habit-encrusted outer shell of words, a maker of Cornell collages from the materials of perception and recollection.

It is not usual for a poet of Muldoon's years to have not only an *oeuvre*—eight volumes of poetry, as well as numerous chapbooks, plays, and children's books—but an *oeuvre* disclosing significant shifts and evolutions. But Muldoon, more than most, is an artist

in high flight from self-repetition and the deadening business of living up to created expectations. His books seem always to be in reaction to the work that has gone before, though not in an arbitrary and willed way, but in a way of testing, pushing hard at latent elements, and exploring hints dropped in earlier poems. Thus we see the balanced take on the unemphatic daily in *New Weather* (1973) open out to the more engaged social and political querying of *Mules* (1977); the transitional *Why Brownlee Left* (1980) ushers in the more subjectively idiosyncratic *Quoof* (1983), with its ramped-up wordplay and more venturesome rhyming. *Meeting the British* (1987) showcases, in "7, Middagh Street," Muldoon's gift for eccentric impersonation, as he imagines himself inside the language-skin of figures like W. H. Auden, Louis Mac-Niece, Carson McCullers, and others who passed through Auden's *ménage à terre*. *Madoc: A Mystery* (1986) plays out a complex historical imagining, in the words of reviewer Lucy McDiarmid, "what might have happened if the Romantic poets Robert Southey and Samuel Taylor Coleridge had indeed come (as they planned in 1794) to America and created a 'pantisocracy' ('equal rule for all') on the banks of the Susquehanna River in Pennsylvania." I suspect, only half in jest, that Muldoon fastened on the subject so that he could work some acrobatic variations on that most beautiful word, "Susquehanna."

With *The Annals of Chile* (1994) and *Hay* (1998), we see the needle of the work flinging back toward center, preserving the *outré* rhymes and venturesome asides, but returning to a more personal and emotionally exposed subject matter, as in the tour-de-force long poem "Incantata" that closes *The Annals of Chile.* There is the sense, in these later books, that the poet has drawn the circle wide and returned, interesting in view of the fact that since 1987 he has made his home in the U.S. (he teaches at Princeton University) and is a U.S. citizen.

Or maybe it's not so interesting after all. Maybe these plate shifts on the outer crust have little or nothing to do with the chthonic element, which is all about language and memory and may well obey laws of its own.

Muldoon has noted somewhere, in interview, that he first began writing poems as a way to get around a certain teacher's weekly essay requirement, an easy way, that is, and if one wonders anything about the evolution of this poet's art, it has to be something like: What happened between the initial presumption of ease and the realization that must underwrite any serious writer's perseverance in the face of the extraordinary difficulty of getting the words to stick to the page? The business gets more interesting when we remark the contradiction between the casual-seeming surface—the unemphatic rhythms that tighten suddenly around some image or offbeat association, the details extracted as if by crow's beak from the realms of the overlooked—and the prodigious, patient labor that goes (by admission) into their making.

I don't believe that there is any commonsensical explanation for how this all works. I would go, rather, to the poet's own assertion—that part of the magic of writing poetry is that "one knows as little as possible" about what one is doing. But such a profession of ignorance is not so much a retreat of intellect before the mysteries, an abjuration of responsibility, as it is a hard-fought metaphysical alignment of self to language and perception, a clearing away of expectations and the myriad comfort-giving templates that tell the poet what the poem should be before the poem itself has had a say in the matter.

Yes, this makes it sound as if Muldoon is a language mystic, a believer in annunciations and threads of inspiration. Queried about this, he responded: "I do absolutely think of it"—the process of writing—"as a mystical experience." Composition, he avers, is a kind of divination. Muldoon speaks of giving himself over "to the force of language, for which one is a conduit or medium." He does add, however, that "the 'divining' metaphor breaks down in the sense that the rod is at once unknowing... and absolutely *knowing*. In other words, all the intelligence one can muster (and probably some that one can't) needs to be brought to bear on making sense of precisely what it is that is being divined."

This may seem like a somewhat recondite reflection from a poet so thoroughly immersed in the immediacies of the immanent, the detail-nubbled surface of the world. Then, moreover, there is the admission—this from the master of the windfall *trouvé*—that Muldoon's favorite poets, the poets who "continue to matter most," are Donne, Byron, Keats, Frost, and Yeats.[1] How do we explain the obscure propagation of taste and influence in any writer's work?

In Muldoon's case—and of course I'm guessing—it seems a steady confrontation between the irresistible force of what has been done and the immovable determination to not repeat or echo the work of the past. For the sounds and verbal connivings of the masters are precisely what stands in the way of the fresh perception.

In the opening lines of "The Mudroom," the long poem that opens Muldoon's most recent collection, *Hay*, the poet writes:

> We followed the narrow track, my love, we followed the
> narrow
> track through a valley in the Jura
> to where the goats delight to tread upon the brink
> of meaning. I carried my skating rink,
> the folding one, plus
> a pair of skates laced with convolvulus,
> you a copy of the feminist Haggadah,
> from last year's Seder. I reached for the haggaday

> or hasp over the half door of the mudroom
> in which, by and by, I grasped the rim
> not of a quern or a chariot wheel but a wheel
> of Morbier propped like the last reel
> of *The Ten Commandments* or *The Robe.*

Reading, slipping in and out of comprehension like a feverish patient slipping in and out of adjoining dreams, I think: "For better or worse—mostly better—this poem, this book, could not have been written by anyone else writing in English today, or ever." If one of the triumphs of poetic voice is perfect originality in the wedding of perception to diction, then Muldoon has indeed triumphed. Here is the utterly credible wobble of the speaking voice, the easy melding of a lightly undertaken lyric convention—"We followed the narrow track, my love"—with the poker-faced subversion of that high address—"I carried my skating rink, / the folding one"—chased by a sudden drop into the obscurantist maneuvers that only the deepest spelunking rhymer could fetch forth. I love it, the sense I have of being poised between vastly divergent registers of feeling—between bemused ironic detachment and the drive-by recognition of profundity (always there in the work); how the sound of a word can, mid-line, tip us one way or another. I love the determined tethering of sense to the progress of the outlandish matings ("Haggadah"/"haggaday"), the etymological surprises ("haggaday," "quern") that are like little Advent windows into the suddenly cavernous house of language.

Yet I heed, too, the image of the goats who "delight to tread upon the brink / of meaning," for it describes something of my feeling as a reader, that the downside of Muldoon's exciting brinkmanship is that I quite often find myself treading the fine line between what feels like a strikingly subtle apprehension and what could easily pass for non-sense, which I will maintain is different from nonsense. Not that Muldoon's lines cannot almost always be pursued into some ultimately precise signification, but on these occasions I speak of the forensics-caliber labors of figuring out are not repaid by that which is figured out.

Example. Here is a passage from the same poem, a few lines farther along. Muldoon writes:

> There a wheel felloe of ash or sycamore
> from the quadriga to which the steeds had no sooner been
>   hitched
> than it foundered in a blue-green ditch
> with the rest of the Pharaoh's
> war machine was perfectly preserved between two
>   amphoras,
> one of wild birdseed, the other of Kikkoman.
> It was somewhere in this vicinity that I'd hidden the
>   afikomen
> at last year's Seder.

I delight, as always, in the uncanniness, the adventuring stretch, but I also become aware that I am not so much reading a poem of insidiously complex intent as I am testing myself on a cunning obstacle course, viewing the mere wresting forth of sense a sufficient achievement.

But this path of higher risk is Muldoon's way out and way forward. It is a following out of implications latent in the work at least since *Quoof,* and the effect on the poetry culture has been tonic. Muldoon has moved the fall-line, giving poets everywhere a new sense of permission about rhyme and narrative logic, not to mention scale and surface texture. Influence moves first, I think, by way of sound and rhythm. The influencer, like some influenza, creating in fellow poets a restlessness—the old words do not want to rest on the page like they used to—as well as a quickening, as from something unforeseen in the breeze. On top of his many achievements—through them—Paul Muldoon is just such an influencer.

Sven Birkerts is the author of Readings *and* The Gutenberg Elegies: The Fate of Reading in an Electronic Age, *and the editor of* Graywolf Forum One: Tolstoy's Dictaphone: Technology and the Muse. *He teaches at Mount Holyoke College and is a member of the core faculty of the Bennington Writing Seminars.*

---

1 The list of Muldoon's influences and favorite writers is not, of course, confined to these five poets who all have five letters in their last names. In written response to this interviewer's questions, he also cited the prose of Sterne, Melville, Joyce, and Stevenson. "*Treasure Island* is one of my very favorite books. I'd love to be able to write something like that." Also mentioned

favorably were Ashbery and Simic. But the real revelation—and delight—to me was the poet's genuinely serious regard for some of our leading songwriters. I was responding to a pair of lines in the poem "I'm Your Man" in *Hay,* in which Muldoon offers, apropos Leonard Cohen: "his songs have meant far more to me / than most of the so-called poems I've read." Asked about this, he responded: "It does seem a little excessive, I suppose, but I'm going to stick to it. I'd say 'Suzanne' or 'Bird on the Wire' or 'Joan of Arc' are much better constructed, are built to withstand more pressure per square inch, than most poetry we meet in most magazines and, alas, find collected in most slim volumes. . . . Cohen has a fine ear, too, something that's rare enough even among quite highly respected poets. So, I'd go so far as to say that, despite the fact that they're involved in a project which is not strictly 'literary,' writers like Leonard Cohen or Bob Dylan or Bruce Springsteen or Paul Simon or Joni Mitchell or Warren Zevon score an extraordinarily high number of successes. The fact that they *are* involved in musical enterprises to boot means that they are likely to 'mean far more,' if only because one's more likely to be exposed to them. There's nothing strange about this, I think. Nothing mysterious. It's a function of the impact of popular culture, particularly on the second half of the twentieth century, and it's one of the reasons my comment on Cohen might seem not in the least excessive to many people of my generation." [2]

[2] Yes, I know that David Foster Wallace does this all the time, but I frankly couldn't think of another way to work in the to-me-fascinating fact that Muldoon—picture it—plays the electric guitar, about which he writes: "I've got one in the basement, along with a very impressive range of effects boxes which allow me to harbor the illusion that I sound half decent. The fact that Leonard Cohen has gone *off* the road prompts me to think there might be a place for me *on* it, I suppose, so I'm working towards that end."

SIX FIGURES *A novel by Fred G. Leebron. Knopf, $22.00 cloth. Reviewed by Stewart O'Nan.*

Fred G. Leebron's provocative second novel takes on the frustrations of the young American middle class, born to privilege and fearful they may fail in their expected pursuit of success. By painstakingly dissecting the thwarted aspirations of its main character, Warner Lutz, it serves as a cautionary tale for the Nasdaq generation.

Warner is in nonprofit fundraising, and feels he's been outstripped by his contemporaries, already enjoying Porsches and exotic vacations. Though he's in the business of helping the poor, he can't stop dreaming of the material comforts his background and education seem to promise. "Yet he still wanted more. Every morning when he drove Sophie in their shitcan hundred-thousand-plus-mile Honda with the guardrail crease down one side to the private but only $175-a-month preschool and he saw the other parents in their new Volvos and minivans and Suburbans, he wanted more."

The Lutzes are newly moved with their two children to Charlotte, North Carolina, a boomtown awash in conspicuous consumption. Warner's wife, Megan, latches onto a hardly paying job at a gallery that specializes in corporate art—a job that nonetheless threatens Warner's sense of self, as he has to remind himself that he still makes ten thousand more than she does.

As in Chuck Palahniuk's *Fight Club*, everything in *Six Figures* has a price tag, a value as a status symbol. Warner desperately aspires to this materialism, even feels anger at those who have achieved it ahead of him. "Perhaps his negativism was devolving through envy into insanity, but you couldn't fail to see, no matter how much you tried, the quick doubling of the stock market, the decline of mortgage rates, the ascent of salaries of nearly everyone you knew—your mother, your siblings, your college and graduate school classmates—into the land of six figures."

Six Figures is about desire, about unfulfilled expectations and how they eat away at a person. Warner is dissatisfied with everything in his life. He gets no respect at work, their daughter, Sophie, is judged to be slow by their daycare, and Megan wants a house they can't afford. When his job at the nonprofit organization MORE is jeopardized through no real fault of his own, he begins to implode. He's intelligent and hardworking; he *deserves* better than this. At home, the smaller frustrations of watching the children drive him further within himself.

And then, without warning, someone attacks Megan at the gallery. It's unclear who. She and Warner had just argued bitterly, and Warner took off in the car with the children, saying he'd take them to the lake. But he didn't take them to the lake; he angrily made a U-turn as the scene closed.

The arrival of violence midway through the book changes the stakes of *Six Figures*. Where before we were watching the slow erosion of a man and his family, now we await the outcome of what seems to be a mystery. Will Megan recover? Will she end up brain-damaged? Her mother suspects Warner, as do the police. Warner's parents come down to Charlotte as well, and the friction between all the parties involved brings up unresolved issues from the past—revelations of domestic violence and sexual infidelity that may figure into the mix. The issues so clearly outlined in the beginning exposition give way to a different kind of inquiry.

This is all done in short, succinct takes, jump-cutting between the major characters. At first, Warner is given center stage, but as the book progresses, the author spreads the narration around, somewhat diluting his effect. The hateful relationships uncovered by the introduction of the parents tend to be a bit thin and melodramatic, not as rich as the earlier sections.

But what audacity Leebron has, dealing with what might be seen, in this age of heartwarming novels, as unsympathetic, even ugly-spirited characters. Listen to Warner, ruminating about the woman who has labeled Sophie as slow: "He knew who Mary was. She was the fat bitch with the tree-trunk legs and the barn-sized behind. She wore a lot of denim, and her big fat face had thin judgmental lips and patronizing eyes set behind schoolteacher glasses." Greed and anger are merely symptoms of a larger spiritual sickness. Warner and Megan, in their selfishness, in their self-absorption and belief in themselves as special and deserving, are reminiscent of Frank and April Wheeler of Richard Yates's great *Revolutionary Road.*

Their fate is less dire than that of the Wheelers, however. The attack on Megan, rather than complicating their previous issues, dispenses with them, clears the air. The cautionary tale works its magic, and in the end the main characters (and their fortunes) are deeply changed, but not before *Six Figures* has shown us the squirmy underside of middle-class ambition.

Stewart O'Nan's most recent novel is A Prayer for the Dying *(Henry Holt). In June, Doubleday will publish his nonfiction history* The Circus Fire, *and in September, Atlantic will release a new novel,* Everyday People.

THE CARTOGRAPHER'S VACATION *Poems by Andrea Cohen. Owl Creek Press, $13.00 paper. Reviewed by David Daniel.*

With its aesthetic roots planted in the tradition of American Surrealism, Andrea Cohen's first collection, *The Cartographer's Vacation,* is delightfully unfashionable. Cohen might well have hung these lines from her poem "Instructions for Writing" on the cover of the book: "Don't let facts / distract you / from the truth"— lines which seem both to guide her and to distinguish this interesting volume from most of her contemporaries, who tend to support their poems on autobiographical data rather than imaginative vision. While Cohen does, if somewhat elliptically, trace a specific familial history, more importantly, as the title suggests, she attempts to map and then navigate a dignified, coherent course among the contingencies of destiny.

The first of the book's three sections focuses on the narrator's childhood; these poems summon up a ghostly world in which the losses of the past haunt the present, and in which the present, too, seems to haunt and revise the past with its wisdom. In "Memory," Cohen conjures the absent mother as it begins: "Quietly the snow begins / falling filling / the windowsill / like a glass / of milk our mother / is pouring." "How long ago," the poem continues, "she began.... We expected her task / to take forever...." It didn't. An entire house is being auctioned: "Save the one window / we kneel before / fingers plugging our ears / fending off the shackling / laughter of the wealthy snowmaker / and his machinery / for which we pawned / our tongues / for which we'd pay anything." While this borders on sentimentality, a charge to which this section is particularly vulnerable, the strangeness of Cohen's imagination—the surprise, for instance, of the word "machinery"—gives sinew to the sentiment; this strength, evident in a number of poems, allows her to explore sentimental territory gracefully.

However effective many of the early poems are, the book improves a good deal in the second and third sections, in which the work turns more outward and Cohen's spirits seem to gather flesh. This earthliness anchors her extravagant imagination, allowing a much broader, subtler range of expression; many of these poems are ambitious, richly ambiguous, and wonderfully witty. In "Calendar Maker"—one of a number of persona poems—the narrator states, "I predict nothing / but merely load the dates / like bullets / in narrow chambers." One of the calendars lands in the office of a young mechanic who "yanks Miss April / from her nail" when he sees a young woman, his wife-to-be, it turns out, approaching, "with an open map / and a question / he'll take / a lifetime answering." Whether the accidents of the future hold a bullet or a lifetime of love, Cohen at this point in the book has clearly decided to resist the lure—suggested in the first section—of a dimly lit past, embracing the darkness that lays ahead: "When you look ahead, / think of Lot's wife, / when you look back, / think of Lot" ("Instructions for Writing").

In the final, and perhaps best, poem, "In the Cemetery," the narrator, driving "undestined until a cemetery / pulls up," discovers "My name's not here, / but scattered across the country." After a moving, darkly funny litany of people and places, she evokes finally the "anonymous on another continent, / ashes lost in a countryside / I've visited only briefly, / eating sachertorte, sampling schnapps." She then seems tempted to rest among the dead surrounding her, where the grass, grown taller, "might hide me if I stopped." With characteristic dignity, she does not stop: "What's left of my family / has enough to mourn, / and in a kitchen nearby, / someone is waiting for supper." Continuing the admirable tradition of small presses publishing books that are somewhat out of step with current fashion, Owl Creek Press deserves great credit: *The Cartographer's Vacation* is a serious, unusual, and often beautiful book.

EQUAL LOVE *Stories by Peter Ho Davies. Mariner Books/Houghton Mifflin, $12.00 paper. Reviewed by Michael Byers.*

In Peter Ho Davies's second collection, *Equal Love,* common domestic situations give rise, in unexpected ways, to moments of luminous reflection. Davies's stories are allusive, mysterious, often funny, and tender. As in his debut collection, *The Ugliest House in the World,* Davies continues to be a meticulous, imaginative craftsman whose work is polished at every level. In "Brave Girl," we see a dentist's office, and its back room, "a tiny cubicle intended for gas extractions but rarely used by my father... There was still a high bed, upholstered in blistered red vinyl, and a tall stainless steel instrument tray which I could use as a desk." And in the shop of Mr. Pang, who builds grave goods for Chinese funerals, we see "white paper furniture, and further back life-size paper suits hanging on the wall."

The strongest stories in the book, "Small World" and "Equal Love," are about love, and lust, between people who shouldn't be falling in love or having sex. Risk and infidelity are always reliable materials, but Davies views them with his own humane eye, presenting good, mostly likeable people, aware of their frailties, who are nonetheless apt to do nasty things. When the married Wilson, in "Small World," goes to Boston for an actuarial conference and discovers that his high school sweetheart, Joyce, still lives in the city, he arranges to meet her. Wilson's wife back home is in her third trimester of pregnancy. He knows he shouldn't go see this old flame, but he does. "Something about the odds of it, he decides, the odds of his being here, of her still being in town, of its really being her, makes it feel implacably innocent—not like a choice, more like an accident of fate." How plausible this sounds! Later that night, when Wilson and Joyce end up parked by a frozen pond, the comical awkwardness of the car "makes it seem less serious, not like faithlessness, not like betrayal, not like sex, at least not until it's over and the car windows are fogged and they pull their clothes on again. Or perhaps having started, neither of them has the heart to stop." The story is—like much of *Equal Love*—sad, lovely, and a little frightening.

In many of these stories we get only a gesture toward resolution. Davies, for the most part, allows his situations to speak for themselves. In "Today Is Sunday," for example, a son and his middle-aged father drive off to the nursing home to visit the father's extremely senile mother. In a moment of confusion, the grandmother addresses the son as the father, sounding a chord of unease in the younger man. But the story ends with the father and son discussing their smoking habits on the drive home. It's a tender, meaningful exchange, but it's lightly handled, and what could have been a weighty moment turns out not to be. The story, as a result, feels pleasantly unbuilt—nicely incidental, and memorable not for any ostentatious architecture but for its acuity of observation and its smooth, confident movement. In two other stories, where the resolutions are less glancing ("Cakes of Baby" and "Frogmen"), the stories end as though with a sudden sharp noise—surprising, but fitting in both instances.

It is, finally, Davies's range that is most impressive. The chorus of voices in *Equal Love* is more diverse than in any collection in recent memory: we read stories from the point of view of a middle-aged black postman in 1960's New Hampshire, a ten-year-old English boy, a Chinese-American publishing scion in San Francisco, a laid-off English encyclopedia salesman, and a drug-addled new mother in Oregon. Every one of these voices rings entirely true, testament to Davies's perfect ear. Peter Ho Davies's own voice—gentle, lucid, assured—is an indispensable one.

Michael Byers is the author of the story collection The Coast of Good Intentions. *His most recent story in* Ploughshares, *"The Beautiful Days," has been selected for an O. Henry Award.*

*Books Recommended by
Our Advisory Editors*

Russell Banks recommends *Harbor Lights,* a novel by Theodore Weesner: "Ted Weesner, over the years since his powerful first novel, *The Car Thief,* has come numerous times to the rescue of American realism in fiction, and he's done it again with *Harbor Lights,* a tough-minded and compassionate portrait of a good man struggling against odds not to hurt the people he loves." (Atlantic Monthly)

Jane Hirshfield recommends *The Dumbbell Nebula,* poems by Steve Kowit: "A book of rangy, big-hearted, capacious poems, full of surprising wisdoms and affection for the world as it is." (Heyday)

Maxine Kumin recommends *The Making of a Poem,* an anthology edited by Mark Strand and Eavan Boland: "An eminently sensible book to work from, this anthology of poetic forms is delightfully varied, with succinct commentary." (Norton)

James Alan McPherson recommends *Billy Verité,* a novel by Rick Harsch: "A portrait of La Crosse, Wisconsin, and the human condition, in late twentieth-century America, from an absolutely original point of view." (Steerforth)

Maura Stanton recommends *Liver,* poems by Charles Harper Webb: "*Liver,* winner of the Felix Pollak Prize in Poetry, is a book you can read cover to cover with astonishing delight. The poems are witty, imaginative, stylistically sophisticated, and completely accurate about life on a planet crowded with billions of others like you. Buy this book!" (Wisconsin)

Dan Wakefield recommends *In the Family Way,* a novel by Lynne Sharon Schwartz: "*In the Family Way* is a witty, loving, totally credible novel of the way a typically atypical family lives now. Another fine novel by the author of that small masterpiece, *Leaving Brooklyn.*" (Morrow)

*New Books by
Our Advisory Editors*

Mary Gordon, *Seeing Through Places: Reflections on Geography and Identity,* a memoir: Eight beautiful essays map out the places that have shaped Gordon's life and writing, from her grandmother's house to a Cape Cod writer's retreat to her Manhattan apartment. (Scribner)

Marilyn Hacker, *Squares and Courtyards,* poems: Precise, haunting, elegant, and elegiac, Hacker's ninth volume celebrates her community of friends in Paris and New York and their courage as they live with HIV and cancer. (Norton)

DeWitt Henry, *Breaking Into Print,* an anthology: Collecting first and early stories from *Ploughshares* by writers who are now literary lights, Henry serves up an invaluable reference for new writers. Headnotes for each story and interleafed shoptalk make this a sparkling commentary on craft. (Beacon)

Bill Knott, *Laugh at the End of the World: Collected Comic Poems 1969–1999:* Knott's tenth volume gathers three decades of virtuoso poems, showcasing his iconoclastic wit, his unique view of the world, and his fiercely original language, proving Marvin Bell was right when he said that Knott can "twist the neck of syntax until it turns blue." (BOA)

James Alan McPherson, *A Region Not Home: Reflections from Exile,* essays: With topics ranging from racism in the South to Disneyland, McPherson provocatively probes the geography of a morally bankrupt society, as he yearns for "spiritual civility." Often magical and transcendent, all of these essays are heartfelt and resonant. (Simon & Schuster)

Leonard Michaels, *A Girl with a Monkey: New and Selected Stories:* This collection of Michaels's fiction from the early sixties to nineties glows with his inimitable style and trenchant perspectives on love and sex. (Mercury)

Robert Pinsky, *Jersey Rain,* poems: Marking a fresh, lyrical direction in Pinsky's work, this volume is a luminous, fugue-like meditation on the themes of a life guided by Hermes: deity of music and deception, escort of the dead, inventor of instruments, the brilliant messenger and trickster of heaven. (FSG)

Charles Simic, *Jackstraws,* poems: This collection of new poems paints exquisite and shattering word pictures that lend meaning to a chaotic world, uniting the solemn with the absurd. Simic continues to startle with images of the ethereal, fantastic visions of the everyday, and moments full of humor and heartache. (FSG)

Gerald Stern, *Last Blue,* poems: A statement from Stern himself illuminates the focus of his outstanding twelfth collection: "Light vs. darkness has always been one of my themes, but now more than ever. Not only is this the root—and metaphor—for all the major religions, but the almost biological frame of reference for humans. With me, it is overwhelming, personal." (Norton)

Mark Strand, *The Weather of Words: Poetic Invention,* essays: A brilliant and witty collection of writings on the art and nature of poetry, exploring the relationship between photographs and poems, the eternal lyric, old forms, and an alphabet of influences. (Knopf)

Ellen Bryant Voigt, *The Flexible Lyric,* essays: These eloquent essays celebrate the art and craft of lyric poetry, passionately and astutely revisiting the work of poets from Shakespeare to Bishop. The book is an inspired argument, proving that the making of poems is not just a trade but a calling. (Georgia)

Derek Walcott, *Tiepolo's Hound,* poems: Published with twenty-five full-color reproductions of Walcott's own paintings, *Tiepolo's Hound* is a stunning book-length poem that is at once the spiritual biography of Camille Pissarro, a history in verse of Impressionist painting, and a memoir of Walcott's desire to catch the visual world in more than words. (FSG)

CALLING ALL PLOUGHSHARES WRITERS If you have been published in *Ploughshares* and have not heard from us recently about participating in our Web project, please send your current address to us by mail or e-mail (authors@emerson.edu).

SURVEY RESULTS Thanks to all of the subscribers who filled out our reader survey, which was mailed last fall to 3,674 individuals in the U.S. selected from our subscription list. We happily received 797 responses—more than we had anticipated. As many people surmised from the nature of the questions, we are planning to expand our Web site (http://www.emerson.edu/ploughshares). The Web development project is being funded by a grant from the Lila Wallace–Reader's Digest Fund, and the new site will be launched in the fall of 2001. Yet, contrary to some readers' fears, we will continue to print *Ploughshares* in its present form; the Web site will be a supplement, not a replacement, for the existing journal.

Indeed, readers seem quite satisfied with the magazine as it is— the guest-editor format, the balance of works—although they are, in general, more partial to fiction than to poetry or nonfiction. They are voracious readers, of course, with 38% perusing more than twenty books of fiction a year, and 39% reading at least ten books of poetry. They are just as apt to buy their books online as they are in an independent or chain bookstore. Journals, however, are still typically ordered through the mail. Most first saw or heard about *Ploughshares* in a bookstore, through direct mail, or by word of mouth. *Ploughshares* also has a fairly strong pass-along value, with 88% of subscriber copies being read by friends or family. Our subscribers read many, many other magazines, citing 245 different literary titles and 340 commercial publications. *Story, Glimmer Train,* and *Poets & Writers* topped the literary list, and *The New Yorker, Harper's,* and *The Atlantic Monthly* headed the commercial list.

As expected, our readers have a strong creative writing bent or association: a total of 83% have participated in a writing program, conference, or class, either as students or teachers. Seventy-four percent have submitted manuscripts to magazines, 36% to *Ploughshares.* Demographically, 59% of our readers are female. Forty-eight percent are in the 35–54 age brackets, and 35% are over fifty-five. Ninety-two percent have bachelor's degrees or better, and 55% chose literature or creative writing as their main course of study. Twenty-four percent are writers by profession, and 20% are educators. Twenty-six percent have annual household incomes of $100,000 or more, 93% are Caucasian, and almost all are U.S. citizens. We have subscribers in every state: 41% in the Northeast, 19% in the South, 18% in the Midwest, and 22% in the West. The states with the most readers are Massachusetts (16%), California (13%), and New York (12%).

Eighty-two percent currently have Internet access, mostly from home, with an additional 15% expecting to be online within a year. Seventy-five percent check their e-mail daily, although they surf the Web less frequently. Since going online, 33% buy more books, yet 11% purchase fewer newspapers. Mostly they find Web sites through search engines and links; banner ads have almost no effect. When they search for literary subjects, sixty-six percent are looking for articles about authors, books, and writing, rather than for actual works of poetry or fiction. If they come across works of interest, 78% will read poems online immediately, but 89% will either print or bookmark stories to read later. Our subscribers listed 171 different literary Web sites that they visit, with *Poetry Daily, Salon,* and *Poets & Writers* on top. Of the 227 different non-literary sites mentioned, Amazon.com, *The New York Times,* and Yahoo! were the most popular. The features they'd most like to see on an expanded *Ploughshares* Web site are: literary news, stories and poems from past issues, submitting and writing tips, extensive literary links, book recommendations, and live chats with authors and editors. Hardly anyone would be willing to pay even a nominal fee to access these features, however.

These results were tabulated by John Andrews of D. Hilton Associates in Texas. The full report is available on our Web site at http://www.emerson.edu/ploughshares/survey.html.

CONTRIBUTORS' NOTES

Spring 2000

WILLIAM ALLEN is the author of *Sevastopol: On Photographs of War* (Xenos, 1997) and *The Man on the Moon* (NYU, 1987). An artist and teacher at NYU, the Cooper Union, and the School of Visual Arts, he now works at Salve Regina University in Newport, Rhode Island.

NIN ANDREWS is the author of *The Book of Orgasms* (Cleveland State) and *Spontaneous Breasts* (Pearl). She is currently editing a collection of Henri Michaux translations (Cleveland State).

MARY JO BANG's book, *Apology for Want,* received the Bakeless Prize. She is the poetry co-editor of *Boston Review* and a Hodder Fellow at Princeton University. Her poems have appeared recently or are forthcoming in *The New Republic, The Yale Review, The Paris Review, The Kenyon Review,* and *Volt.*

RUSSELL BANKS is the author most recently of the novels *Cloudsplitter* and *Rule of the Bone.* "Quality Time" will appear in his forthcoming collection of new and selected stories, *The Angel on the Roof: The Stories of Russell Banks,* in June from HarperCollins.

MARY BEHRENS lives in Boston and is on the faculty of Montserrat College of Art in Beverly, Massachusetts. She is represented in Boston by the Creiger-Dane Gallery and in Provincetown, Massachusetts, by the DNA Gallery. Her most recent solo exhibition, *The Far & Away,* was in March 2000 at Creiger-Dane.

CATHY BOWMAN is the author of two collections of poetry, *Rock Farm* and *1-800-HOT RIBS,* which was recently reprinted as part of the Carnegie Mellon Classic Contemporary Poetry Series. She teaches at Indiana University in Bloomington.

CHRISTOPHER CAHILL is the author of a novel, *Perfection,* which was published in Paris by L'Age d'Homme.

LAN SAMANTHA CHANG is the author of *Hunger: A Novella and Stories.* Her fiction has appeared in *Story, The Atlantic Monthly, The Best American Short Stories,* and elsewhere. She is an Alfred Hodder Fellow at Princeton University, where she is at work on a novel.

TINA CHANG received an M.F.A. in poetry from Columbia University. Her work has appeared in *Quarterly West, The Missouri Review,* and *The Indiana Review,* and has been anthologized in *Identity Lessons* and *Poetry Nation.* She has received awards from the Academy of American Poets, *Poets & Writers,* Villa Montalvo, and Fundación Valparaíso.

KILLARNEY CLARY is the author of *By Common Salt* (Oberlin, 1996); *Who Whispered Near Me* (Farrar, Straus & Giroux, 1989, and Bloodaxe Books, England, 1993); and the chapbook *By Me, By Any, Can and Can't Be Done* (Greenhouse Review, 1980). She received a literary fellowship from the Lannan Foundation in 1992, and lives in Los Angeles.

STEVEN CRAMER is the author of three collections of poems, *The Eye that Desires to Look Upward* (1987), *The World Book* (1992), and *Dialogue for the Left and Right Hand* (1997). The poem in this issue, "Goodbye to the Orchard," is the title poem of his fourth collection, which he will soon complete.

JOHN D'AGATA's first collection, *Halls of Fame*, will be published by Graywolf Press in January 2001.

CLAIRE DAVIS teaches fiction at Lewis-Clark State College in Lewiston, Idaho. Her stories have appeared in *The Gettysburg Review, The Southern Review, Shenandoah,* and other magazines. Her first novel, *Winter Range,* is forthcoming from Picador USA this fall. She is at work on another novel.

MEREDITH DRUM lives in Williamsburg, Brooklyn, where she works in a bar. This is her first publication.

DAVID FRANCIS holds M.F.A. and Ph.D. degrees in poetry from the University of Washington and has taught writing and literature at schools in Delaware, Washington, Kentucky, and Poland (Fulbright, 1998). Currently he co-edits *Archaeology in Washington* and teaches at Cornish College of the Arts in Seattle.

DAISY FRIED's first book of poems, *She Didn't Mean To Do It,* won the 1999 Agnes Lynch Starrett Prize, and will be published by the University of Pittsburgh Press this October. A recent Pew Fellow in poetry, her poems have appeared in *The American Poetry Review, The Antioch Review, The Threepenny Review,* and other journals.

JONATHAN GALASSI's second collection of poems, *North Street,* was recently published by HarperCollins.

DOUGLAS GOETSCH is the author of *Nobody's Hell* (Hanging Loose, 1999) and *Wherever You Want* (Pavement Saw, 1997). His honors include a Paumanok Award and an NYFA poetry fellowship. His poems, essays, and reviews have appeared or are forthcoming in *The Iowa Review, Poetry, Hanging Loose, ONTHEBUS, The Fourth Genre,* and online at *Poetry Daily.*

STUART GREENHOUSE is a Ph.D. candidate at the University of Massachusetts, Amherst. His poems have recently appeared or are forthcoming in *Fence, Grand Street, The Notre Dame Review, The Paris Review,* and *The Wallace Stevens Journal.*

JOHN HOPPENTHALER's poetry has recently appeared or is forthcoming in *Tar River Poetry, Chelsea, Connecticut Review, The Bloomsbury Review, Luna,* and *Clockpunchers: Poetry of the American Workplace.* His essays, reviews, and interviews appear regularly in such journals as *Arts & Letters, Chelsea,* and *Kestrel,* where he is co-editor.

CYNTHIA HUNTINGTON's poems have appeared or are forthcoming in *The Massachusetts Review, Harvard Review, TriQuarterly,* and *Michigan Quarterly Review.* "The Tempest," an excerpt from her latest book, *The Salt House,* will appear in *American Nature Writers 2000.* She directs the creative writing program at Dartmouth College.

TROY JOLLIMORE has published poetry in several journals, including *The Malahat Review* and *Press,* and has also written for *The Boston Book Review.* He has taught philosophy at Georgetown University and the University of California, Davis, and currently resides in Chico, California.

EDMUND KEELEY is the author of seven novels, nine books of nonfiction, and fourteen volumes of poetry in translation. He taught English and creative writing at Princeton University for forty years. His latest books are *Inventing Paradise: The Greek Journey, 1937–47* (1999) and *On Translation: Reflections and Conversations* (2000).

YUSEF KOMUNYAKAA has published eleven books of poems, including *Neon Vernacular: New and Selected Poems 1977–1989,* which won the 1994 Pulitzer Prize, and *Thieves of Paradise,* a finalist for the 1999 National Book Critics Circle Award. Forthcoming are *Blue Notes: Essays, Interviews & Commentaries, Talking Dirty to the Gods,* and *Pleasure Dome: New and Collected Poems 1975–1999.*

NICOLE KRAUSS has contributed poems to *The Paris Review* and *Western Humanities Review,* and in the U.K. to *Poetry Review* and *PN Review.* Her work was also included in the anthology *New Poetries II* (Carcanet). She recently made a documentary about Joseph Brodsky for BBC Radio 3.

MELISSA KWASNY is a recent graduate of the M.F.A. program in poetry at the University of Montana. She is the author of two novels, most recently *Trees Call for What They Need,* and has poems published or forthcoming in *CutBank, Poetry Northwest, Nimrod, Puerto del Sol,* and *Fine Madness.*

JAMES LASDUN has published two collections of stories, *Delirium Eclipse* and *Three Evenings,* and two books of poetry, *A Jump Start* and *Woman Police Officer in Elevator.* With Michael Hofmann he co-edited the anthology *After Ovid: New Metamorphoses.* His story "The Siege" was adapted by Bernardo Bertolucci for his film *Besieged.*

TIMOTHY LIU was born in 1965. His books of poems are *Vox Angelica, Burnt Offerings,* and *Say Goodnight.* He is also the editor of *Word of Mouth: An Anthology of Gay American Poetry,* forthcoming from Talisman House.

CATE MARVIN's poems have appeared in *New England Review, The Paris Review, Witness,* and other journals, and her fiction is forthcoming in *Gulf Coast.* Currently she is a Ph.D. candidate in English at the University of Cincinnati.

WALT MCDONALD was an Air Force pilot and now teaches writing at Texas Tech University. He has published nineteen collections of poetry and fiction, including *All Occasions* (Notre Dame, forthcoming this September), *Blessings the Body*

Gave (Ohio State, 1998), and others from Massachusetts, Pittsburgh, and Harper & Row. Four books won awards from the National Cowboy Hall of Fame.

KEVIN MCILVOY's novel, *Hyssop*, was published by TriQuarterly Books in 1998 and appeared in paperback (Avon/Bard) in 1999. He has published stories recently in *Chelsea* and *The Southern Review*. For eighteen years he has taught at New Mexico State University, where he is the editor in chief of *Puerto del Sol*.

MELISSA MONROE lives and teaches in New York. *Machine Language*, a collection of her poems, was recently published by Alef Books. The poem in this issue is part of a series suggested by David W. Maurer's study *Whiz Mob: A Correlation of the Technical Argot of Pickpockets with Their Behavior Pattern*.

EMILY MOORE is a 1999 graduate of Princeton University, where she received the Shellabarger Prize Fellowship for her creative thesis, *Dairy*. In 1998, she received a grant from the Barbara Deming Memorial Fund.

TONI MORRISON has written seven novels, most recently *Paradise*, and has been the recipient of the National Book Critics Circle Award, the Pulitzer Prize, and the 1993 Nobel Prize for Literature. She was commissioned to write lyrics for Kathleen Battle and Jessye Norman, and has worked with composers Andre Previn and Richard Danielpour. She is Robert F. Goheen Professor at Princeton University.

ROBERT NAZARENE's poetry appears or is forthcoming in *The Indiana Review*, *Callaloo*, *Nimrod*, *Atlanta Review*, *5 AM*, and other journals. He is a graduate of the Georgetown University School of Business Administration, and lives near St. Louis, Missouri.

JOYCE CAROL OATES is the author most recently of the novel *Blonde* (Ecco/HarperCollins) and the essay collection *Where I've Been, and Where I'm Going* (Dutton). She is a longtime resident of Princeton, New Jersey, where she teaches at the university and helps edit *Ontario Review*.

PEDRO PONCE's fiction has appeared previously in *Gargoyle* and is forthcoming in *Alaska Quarterly Review*. He is a past recipient of a Tara Fellowship for Short Fiction.

SALVATORE QUASIMODO won the Nobel Prize for Literature in 1959.

JAMES RICHARDSON's fifth collection of poems, *How Thing Are*, has just been published by Carnegie Mellon. *Vectors: Aphorisms and Ten-Second Essays* will be out next year. He teaches at Princeton University.

CATIE ROSEMURGY is currently an assistant professor of English at Northwest Missouri State University, where she also co-edits *The Laurel Review*. Her first poetry collection, *My Favorite Apocalypse*, is forthcoming from Graywolf Press. Her poems have appeared in such places as *Michigan Quarterly Review*, *Poetry Northwest*, *Sonora Review*, and *The Best American Poetry 1997*.

J. ALLYN ROSSER's collection of poems, *Bright Moves,* won the Morse Poetry Prize and was published by Northeastern University Press. Her work has recently appeared in *Slate* and *Poetry.* She teaches at Ohio University.

STEPHEN SANDY is the author of seven collections of poetry, most recently *Black Box* (LSU, 1999), *The Thread: New and Selected Poems* (LSU, 1998), and *Thanksgiving Over the Water* (Knopf, 1992). He lives in southern Vermont.

LISA SEWELL's first book of poems, *The Way Out,* was published by Alice James Books in 1998. Recent poems have appeared in *The Massachusetts Review, Shenandoah, Gulf Coast,* and *The American Poetry Review.* A 1999 NEA fellow, she lives in Philadelphia and teaches at Villanova University.

FAITH SHEARIN is an English teacher in Detroit. Her poems have appeared in *Alaska Quarterly Review, New York Quarterly,* and *The Chicago Review,* among others. She was a fellow at the Fine Arts Work Center in Provincetown and writer-in-residence at the Interlochen Arts Academy, and has served on the faculty of the Cranbrook Retreat for Writers. Her work is forthcoming in *The Third Coast: An Anthology of Michigan Poets.*

LAURIE SHECK's most recent book is *The Willow Grove* (Knopf). Recent work is in *The Best American Poetry 2000, The Pushcart Prize 2000, The Kenyon Review, Denver Quarterly, Seneca Review,* and *The Iowa Review.* She currently teaches at Princeton University.

REGINALD SHEPHERD's third book, *Wrong,* was published by the University of Pittsburgh Press in late 1999. Pittsburgh also published his previous two books, *Some Are Drowning* (1993 AWP Award) and *Angel, Interrupted.* He lives in Ithaca, New York, and teaches at Cornell University.

TERESE SVOBODA's most recent book of poetry is *Mere Mortals* (Georgia, 1995). Her most recent book of prose is *Trailer Girl and Other Stories* (Counterpoint, 2000).

BILL SWEENEY lives in New York City and teaches at Collegiate School.

PAULA TATARUNIS's poems have appeared in *The Exquisite Corpse, The Formalist, The Journal of the American Medical Association, The Massachusetts Review, Quarterly West,* and *Poetry.* She received a Massachusetts Cultural Council fellowship grant in 1998, and works as an internist in Medford, Massachusetts.

LYNNE TILLMAN's most recent novel, *No Lease on Life,* was a finalist for the 1998 National Book Critics Circle Award in Fiction. Her history of Books & Co., *Bookstore: The Life and Times of Jeannette Watson and Books & Co.,* was published by Harcourt Brace in October 1999.

ALPAY ULKU's first book of poems, *Meteorology,* was published by BOA Editions in June 1999. His poems have appeared in *The Gettysburg Review, The Malahat Review,* and *Northwest Review,* and are forthcoming in *Witness* and the anthology *American Poetry: The Next Generation.* He works as a technical writer in Chicago.

NANCE VAN WINCKEL is the author of three volumes of poetry: *Bad Girl, With Hawk; After a Spell;* and *The Dirt.* She has also published two collections of short stories, *Limited Lifetime Warranty* and *Quake,* and Persea will bring out a third book, *Curtain Creek Farm,* this June.

A. J. VERDELLE is the author of a novel, *The Good Negress.* She has received fellowships from the Whiting Foundation, the NEA, and the Bunting Institute.

LIZ WALDNER's first book, *Homing Devices,* was published by O Books in 1998; her second, *A Point Is That Which Has No Part,* won the Iowa Poetry Prize for 2000. She is also the author of two chapbooks, *Call* from Meow Press and *With the Tongues of Angels* from Owl Creek Press.

RENÉE & THEODORE WEISS have published and edited the *Quarterly Review of Literature* for almost sixty years. Recently they received a Lifetime Achievement Award from PEN for editing *QRL,* and Theodore Weiss won the 1997 Williams/ Derwood Award for his poetry. They are finishing a joint book of poems.

SUSAN WHEELER's books are *Bag 'o' Diamonds, Smokes,* and the forthcoming novel *Record Palace.* The recipient of a 1999 Guggenheim fellowship, she is teaching this spring at the University of Iowa and in the graduate creative writing program at New School University.

EDMUND WHITE is the author of a dozen books, including *A Boy's Own Story* and biographies of Jean Genet and Marcel Proust. His next novel is *The Married Man* (Knopf, June). He teaches writing at Princeton University.

JULIA WHITTY is a writer and documentary filmmaker living in northern California. Her short fiction has won an O. Henry and the Bernice Slote Award, and was a finalist for the National Magazine Award. Her stories have appeared in *Harper's, Story, The Virginia Quarterly Review, Prairie Schooner, Calyx,* and elsewhere.

C. K. WILLIAMS's most recent books of poetry are *The Vigil* (1997) and *Repair* (1999). A book of essays, *Poetry and Consciousness,* appeared in 1998. A book of autobiographical meditation, *Misgivings,* will be published this April, and *Love Poems and Poems About Love* will be released later in the year. He teaches in the writing program at Princeton University.

THEODORE WOROZBYT is the recipient of grants from the NEA, the Georgia Council for the Arts, and, currently, the Alabama Council on the Arts. His work has recently appeared or is forthcoming in *Green Mountains Review, The Kenyon Review, The North American Review, Prairie Schooner,* and *Sonora Review.*

～

GUEST EDITOR POLICY *Ploughshares* is published three times a year: mixed issues of poetry and fiction in the Spring and Winter and a fiction issue in the Fall, with each guest-edited by a different writer of prominence, usually one whose early work was published in the journal. Guest editors are invited to solicit up to half of their issues, with the other half selected from unsolicited manuscripts screened for them by staff editors. This guest editor policy is designed to introduce readers to different literary circles and tastes, and to offer a fuller representation of the range and diversity of contemporary letters than would be possible with a single editorship. Yet, at the same time, we expect every issue to reflect our overall standards of literary excellence. We liken *Ploughshares* to a theater company: each issue might have a different guest editor and different writers—just as a play will have a different director, playwright, and cast—but subscribers can count on a governing aesthetic, a consistency in literary values and quality, that is uniquely our own.

THE NAME *Ploughshares* 1. The sharp edge of a plough that cuts a furrow in the earth. 2 a. A variation of the name of the pub, the Plough and Stars, in Cambridge, Massachusetts, where the journal *Ploughshares* was founded. 2 b. The pub's name was inspired by the Sean O'Casey play about the Easter Rising of the Irish "citizen army." The army's flag contained a plough, representing the things of the earth, hence practicality; and stars, the ideals by which the plough is steered. 3. A shared, collaborative, community effort that has endured for twenty-nine years. 4. A literary journal that has been energized by a desire for harmony, peace, and reform. Once, that spirit motivated civil rights marches, war protests, and student activism. Today, it still inspirits a desire for beating swords into ploughshares, but through the power and the beauty of the written word.

SUBMISSION POLICIES We welcome unsolicited manuscripts from August 1 to March 31 (postmark dates). All submissions sent from April to July are returned unread. In the past, guest editors often announced specific themes for issues, but we have revised our editorial policies and no longer restrict submissions to thematic topics. Submit your work at any time during our reading period; if a manuscript is not timely for one issue, it will be considered for another. We do not recommend trying to target specific guest editors. Our backlog is unpredictable, and staff editors ultimately have the responsibility of determining for which editor a work is most appropriate. Mail one prose piece and/or one to three poems at a time (mail genres separately). No e-mail submissions. Poems should be individually typed either single- or double-spaced on one side of the page. Prose should be typed double-spaced on one side and be no longer than twenty-five pages. Although we look primarily for short stories, we occasionally publish personal essays/memoirs. Novel excerpts are acceptable if self-contained. Unsolicited book reviews and criticism are not considered. Please do not send multiple submissions of the same genre, and do not send another manuscript until you hear about the first. *No more than a total of two submissions per reading period.* Additional submissions will be returned unread. Mail your manuscript in a page-size manila envelope, your full name and address written on the outside. In general, address submissions to the "Fiction Editor," "Poetry Editor," or "Nonfiction Editor," not to the guest or staff editors by name, unless you have a legitimate association with them or have been previously published in the magazine. Unsolicited work sent directly to a guest editor's home or office will be ignored and discarded; guest editors are formally instructed not to read such work. All manuscripts and correspondence regarding submissions should be accompanied by a self-addressed, stamped envelope (s.a.s.e.) for a response; no replies will be given by e-mail or postcard. Expect three to five months for a decision. We now receive over a thousand manuscripts a month. Do not query us until five months have passed, and if you do, please write to us, including an s.a.s.e. and indicating the postmark date of submission, instead of calling or e-mailing. Simultaneous submissions are amenable as long as they are indicated as such and we are notified immediately upon acceptance elsewhere. We cannot accommodate revisions, changes of return address, or forgotten s.a.s.e.'s after the fact. We do not reprint previously published work. Translations are welcome if permission has been granted. We cannot be responsible for delay, loss, or damage. Payment is upon publication: $25/printed page, $50 minimum per title, $250 maximum per author, with two copies of the issue and a one-year subscription.

SUBSCRIBERS Please feel free to contact us by letter or e-mail with comments, address changes (the post office will not forward journals), or any problems with your subscription. Our e-mail address is: pshares@emerson.edu. Also, please note that on occasion we exchange mailing lists with other literary magazines and organizations. If you would like your name excluded from these exchanges, simply send us an e-mail message or a letter stating so.

SARAH LAWRENCE COLLEGE
SUMMER SEMINARS
FOR WRITERS
June 25-30, 2000

The **Sarah Lawrence College Seminars** provide writers, published and unpublished, with the opportunity to deepen their craft through daily work in small, intensive workshops and in individual meetings with acclaimed poets, fiction and nonfiction writers. Faculty supplement classwork with readings and panel discussions. Academic credit may be earned for these seminars.

Writing is both a calling and a craft.

FICTION

Wesley Brown
Mary LaChapelle
Valerie Martin

NONFICTION

Jo Ann Beard
Jane Bernstein
Mary Morris

POETRY

Laure-Anne Bosselaar
Deborah Digges
Stephen Dobyns
Thomas Lux

Sarah Lawrence College offers an MFA
in Poetry, Fiction and Nonfiction.
For more information, call: Ms. Susan Guma **(914)395-2371** or write:
Sarah Lawrence College, Graduate Studies,
Box PL, 1 Mead Way, Bronxville, NY 10708-5999
e-mail: **grad@mail.slc.edu**

Bewitched Playground

DAVID RIVARD

"What kind of grace rushes through these poems? It makes one joyful, humble, aware, and richer for images one does not forget. It leaves me with a desire to be permanently friends with this mysterious kind of grace." *Tomaz Salamun*

Paperback, $12.95 (1-55597-302-7)

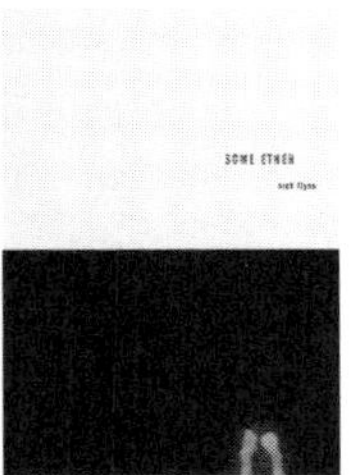

Some Ether

NICK FLYNN

Some Ether is the winner of a "Discovery"/*The Nation* Award and the PEN/Joyce Osterweil Award for Poetry. "These poems are more than testimony; in lyrics of ringing clarity and strange precision, Flynn conjures a will to survive, the buoyant motion toward love which is sometimes all that saves us. *Some Ether* resonates in the imagination long after the final poem; this is a startling, moving debut." *Mark Doty*

Paperback, $12.95 (1-55597-303-5) Available in June

The Stars, the Snow, the Fire

JOHN HAINES

In this wilderness classic, award-winning poet and essayist John Haines, relates his experiences from over twenty years as a homesteader on the Alaskan frontier. As *New York Newsday* has said of his work, "If Alaska had not existed, Haines might well have invented it."

Now in paperback, $15.00 (1-55597-306-X)
Also available as Rocket eBook, $15.00 (1-55597-307-8)

South Wind Changing

JADE NGỌC QUANG HUỲNH

South Wind Changing was named one of five Best Books of the Year by *Time* magazine. Persecuted and forced into a labor camp, South Vietnamese native, Jade Ngọc Quang Huỳnh, shares his riveting experiences of dangerously escaping Vietnam, living in a Thai refugee camp, and starting a new life in the U.S.

Now in paperback, $16.00 (1-55597-305-1) Available in June

THE BOSTON BOOK REVIEW

http://www.BostonBookReview.com

The Best of Both Worlds

The Apollonian

The Bostonian

The Dionysian

The thinking person's literary arts magazine with fiction, poetry, interviews, essays and book reviews.

Subscribe to the BOSTON BOOK REVIEW.
Discover the well-written.

In addition, sign up to receive our **FREE** bimonthly email Gazette for info about authors, new articles and reviews, BBR bestsellers and best picks, occasional short reviews, and more. Send an email with **subscribe** in the subject line to Gazette@soapbox.BostonBookReview.com.

SUBSCRIPTIONS: 1 yr. (10 issues) $24.00
Canada and International add $26.00

plshr

Name ____

Address____

City __________________________ State ______ Zip __________

Credit Card Payments: No. _______________________________
or call (617) 497-0344   Exp. date:____ Signature: ________________

☐ VISA   ☐ MASTERCARD   ☐ DISCOVER   ☐ AMEX

Or send check to:
THE BOSTON BOOK REVIEW, 30 Brattle Street, 4th floor, Cambridge, MA 02138

Conor O'Callaghan:
Seatown and Earlier Poems

"O'Callaghan's poetry is marvellously his own ... [Its] bewitching obliquity ... obviates neat conclusions. What is evident from *Seatown* and its predecessor is that Conor O'Callaghan is a gifted poet." – *The Times Literary Supplement*

March, 2000   96 pages
cloth $19.95   paper $9.95

Nuala Ní Dhomhnaill:
The Water Horse
Poems in Irish with translations by Medbh McGuckian and Eiléan Ní Chuilleanáin

Ní Dhomhnaill's poems easily cross the borders between the mythic and the everyday. Fairies seduce husbands with the latest electronic gadgetry, "Sir Death" is an ebony Adonis, and in his BMW Pluto conveys to the underworld a Persephone with SAD.

"No modern poet in Irish has mined folk material to such advantage." – Gabriel Rosenstock, *The Irish Times*

April, 2000   132 pages
cloth $20.95   paper $12.95

Michael Longley:
The Weather in Japan

With a Zen-like grace, even the briefest poems hurdle logical gaps and sidestep reason to get to truths.

"With each volume Michael Longley publishes, a growing readership delights in the triumphs of his poems. ... Longley's devotees tend to encounter one another with the pleasure that springs from sharing a secret passion." – *Harvard Review*

May, 2000   80 pages
cloth $18.95   paper $9.95

Wake Forest University Press

P.O. Box 7333 • Winston-Salem, NC 27109
phone 336 758-5448 • fax 336 758-5636
e-mail: wfupress@wfu.edu • http://www.wfu.edu/wfupress

the modern writer as witness

Contributors

Marcia Aldrich
Pete Fromm
Dan Gerber
Jean Ross Justice
Julia Kasdorf
Anna Keesey
Maxine Kumin
Thomas Lynch
Joseph McElroy
Roland Merullo
Kent Nelson
Linda Pastan
Maureen Seaton
Floyd Skloot
Paul West

"From its inception, the vision that distinguishes Witness *has been consistent: it is a magazine situated at the intersection of ideas and passions, a magazine energized by the intellect, yet one in which thought is never presented as abstraction, but rather as life blood. Each issue is beautifully produced and eminently readable."*

Stuart Dybek

Call for Manuscripts:

Witness invites submission of memoirs, essays, fiction, poetry and artwork for a special 2000 issue on **Crime in America**.
Deadline: July 15, 2000.

Writings from *Witness* have been selected for inclusion in *Best American Essays, Best American Poetry, Prize Stories: The O. Henry Awards,* and *The Pushcart Prizes.*

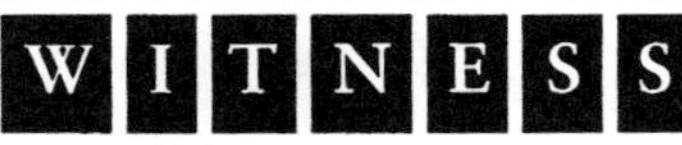

Oakland Community College
Orchard Ridge Campus
27055 Orchard Lake Road
Farmington Hills, MI 48334

Individuals
1 year / 2 issues $15
2 years / 4 issues $28

Institutions
1 year / 2 issues $22
2 years / 4 issues $38

Ploughshares

stories and poems for literary aficionados

Known for its compelling fiction and poetry, *Ploughshares* is widely regarded as one of America's most influential literary journals. Each issue is guest-edited by a different writer for a fresh, provocative slant— exploring personal visions, aesthetics, and literary circles—and contributors include both well-known and emerging writers. In fact, *Ploughshares* has become a premier proving ground for new talent, showcasing the early works of Sue Miller, Mona Simpson, Robert Pinsky, and countless others. Past guest editors include Richard Ford, Derek Walcott, Tobias Wolff, Carolyn Forché, and Rosellen Brown. This unique editorial format has made *Ploughshares,* in effect, into a dynamic anthology series—one that has established a tradition of quality and prescience. *Ploughshares* is published in quality trade paperback in April, August, and December: usually a fiction issue in the Fall and mixed issues of poetry and fiction in the Spring and Winter. Inside each issue, you'll find not only great new stories and poems, but also a profile on the guest editor, book reviews, and miscellaneous notes about *Ploughshares,* its writers, and the literary world. Subscribe today.

Sample *Ploughshares* online: www.emerson.edu/ploughshares

❑ **Send me a one-year subscription for $21.**
I save $8.85 off the cover price (3 issues).

❑ **Send me a two-year subscription for $40.**
I save $19.70 off the cover price (6 issues).

Start with: ❑ Spring ❑ Fall ❑ Winter

Add $5 per year for international. Institutions: $24.

Name ____

Address ____

____

Mail with check to: Ploughshares · Emerson College
100 Beacon St. · Boston, MA 02116